MATADOR

KHALILAH YASMIN

"FIGHT THE BULL."

For Love, Muses, & Consciousness

mat·a·dor
ˈmadəˌdôr/
noun

noun: matador; plural noun: matadors

1. a bullfighter who plays the most important human part in a bullfight.
2. (in ombre, skat, and other card games) any of the highest trumps.

3. he/she who kills the bull.

This is a work of fiction. Names, characters, businesses, places, events and incidents are either the products of the author's imagination or used in a fictitious manner. Any resemblance to actual persons, living or dead, or actual events is purely coincidental.

TABLE OF CONTENTS

PROLOGUE

There's a famous quote by Marcel Proust. It says, "the only real voyage of discovery consists not in seeking new landscapes, but having new eyes." Those words can be interpreted a number of different ways. One thing is for certain, there are things you'll never see because you're not seeing with the other person's eyes. You can be in the same place at the same time and still not have the same perspective of that experience. We not only see with our eyes, our eyes are simply the lens for which images come through. The brain uses past experiences, knowledge, and instinct to decipher the message.

Similarly, we often look at a situation that lacks a backstory and judge the person simply by their actions. We don't often see what led to their actions. The father who robbed a bank because he lost his job and his son needed cancer treatment.

The homeless woman who killed her pimp because he had been beating and manipulating her for several years.

Cause and effect.

The matador also known as the rodeo clown plays an important role in the bull fight. The torero is the basic bull fighter. Unlike the torero, the matador earns his title by finishing the job and killing the bull. Essentially, the two can be the same. A matador is always a torero, but not all toreros can charm the bull with the muleta without being killed themselves. There's definitely an art to it all. .... You know- killing the bull without being killed in the process. Not many have managed it. But those that do, earn the title of being a 'MATADOR'.

Imagine being that bull, repeatedly antagonized after a ritual dance with an audience of thousands cheering for you to win. Or maybe they want the fighter to win, so they are cheering for your demise.

Either way, broken down it's treating a living being like a monster so that living being, the bull, charges towards the bullfighter. Consequently in the end, the animal is killed swiftly with a sword plunged in between the bull's shoulders. This incision goes directly to the animal's heart. The story & dance end with a fatal puncture in this traditional Spanish bullfight.

The hard truth is that the bull just wants to escape. He doesn't want to harm anyone. Like most of us, he just wants to be free.

CHAPTER ONE: THE WOKE, THE SAVAGE, & THE SHADE

It was a rather unusual day in Shanghai. The sky appeared to time lapse very quickly from day to night and then back again. In midst of the chaos in the sky, the iconic 1,500 feet high (OPT) Oriental Pearl Radio & TV Tower stood as the centerpiece in the background. With an immaculate architecture, it stood 19 stories tall, weighing 120,000 tons, fitting up to 2,500 people in the 7 elevators each hour. The OP tower looked like a toy you would find in the NASA gift shop or an antique from a more advanced civilization.

There was a needle at the top lit up like a beacon communicating with another world. There were three sphere structures positioned along the needle giving it the look of a Christmas ornament that only the rich could afford.

Each sphere housed several stories for observation viewing, restaurants, an arcade, an indoor rollercoaster, and museum. The lowest sphere included 7 stories, the higher sphere had 9 stories, and the tallest and smallest sphere close to the needle had 3 stories. In between the sphere structures were 6 observation decks. From a distance the decks looked like magenta diamond clusters on an anniversary bracelet.

The OPT was an iridescent purple, pink, and orange during the day, but at night the tower flickered through several colors the way that blinking Holiday lights flickered in Times Square.

Blue, green, purple, red, yellow, orange, white, and metallic silver frames of light mesmerized all who saw it. The Chinese locals stared as the wide-eyed, lively tourists filmed their every move using hi-tech video equipment interchangeably with iPhones and selfie sticks. Rebecca, Broc, & Parker West were twenty-something siblings whom afforded traveling the world due to the success of their father's Information Technology & Internet franchise MATADOR.

MATADOR gained popularity by creating the first firewall that was impossible to be penetrated through while secretly employing several hackers for similar & contradictory purposes. MATADOR also gained notoriety by spiking views for consumers who want a larger audience for their content but don't necessarily deserve it.

These three siblings ran their own successful internet show 'WOKE, SAVAGE, & THE SHADE' which was titled as monikers for their own personalities, with the help of a MATADOR boost.

WSS highlighted their excessive use of money, power, greed, wasteful spending, live plastic surgery with Rebecca, fucking & ducking unsuspecting women with Broc, and their favorite; 'making fun of the less fortunate, other/darker ethnicities, and those who were different than their upper-class but classless lifestyle'.

Social media once known for being a social place to communicate with others had become a very dark place in recent years. Anything for a few views, shares, and laughs; even if that means demeaning or causing severe damage to others. Nothing is off limits for these three. Views equate to dollars. And in the mind of those who value nothing more, dollars are the only sense that makes any.

Mr. James West, their father was listed as one of Forbes Magazines' Billionaires for the last decade. The only child adopted at birth by a wealthy caucasian family in Santa Barbara who left their fortune to him in their passing. He was built like a traditional football player. Though not very tall, James was strong and firm. His eyes were brown, wide, and curiously always scanning the rooms he was in. He took pride in things like being wealthy, his CIA background, golfing with Donald Trump, government ties, and shitting on the poor.

For the Wests' it didn't matter if the rest of the world was suffering as long as they were financially thriving. And they wanted to make sure you had a front row seat to watch.

Broc (The Savage) was the youngest of the three siblings; blonde, built, and boyishly handsome. Depending on what he was wearing, his eyes mirrored the most beautiful blue an ocean in the tropics had ever seen. His hair flowed to the middle of his back like Tarzan of the new world, if Tarzan wore a leather jacket and rode a motorcycle. He could have been a model but didn't need the clout. Entire convention rooms went silent when Broc entered. Even men stopped to stare. This guy was fucking beautiful and equally just as shallow. He stayed in the gym, chased women, and didn't care whose feelings he hurt. Hedonism personified.

Rebecca AKA Becky (The Shade) was the middle sibling. She prided herself on her long, brown curly hair, butt implants, fake breasts, lip injections, nose job (though she'll say it's for breathing problems), and any other plastic surgery trend to make her look less human and more artificially gorgeous. Ever seen an android you wanted to fuck? Rebecca. The more work she had done, the more she resembled one of those Japanese sex dolls whose faces don't move. If plastic surgeons gave out loyalty cards, she would have her stamps filled every couple of months for never being satisfied with her multiple enhancements. You might think that with so many aims towards perfection, confidence would be implanted as well. But in Rebecca's case, she was just as insecure as she was before she began.

Broc and Rebecca happened to be the result of an affair that their mother Lucy West had with her Italian plastic surgeon Francesco. Not only was Francesco implanting a couple of cubic centimeters of breast enlargement into Lucy, but during several private appointments he implanted every inch of the finest Italian sausage one could find. Mr. West had so many mistresses, he didn't care what Lucy did with her free time and took care of Broc and Rebecca like his own. One redeeming quality...I suppose.

Lucy (mom) immigrated to the United States from a small

town in Slovakia. Naturally beautiful, never needed any work done… but was encouraged by her husband that she should get larger 'tits' if she wanted to keep him entertained. Though in her 50's, she often passed and pretended to be her daughter Rebecca's sister.

Parker (The Woke) is the eldest of the siblings. He had what you call "little man syndrome". You ever seen a tiny chihuahua barking at a Great Dane despite the fact that Great Dane could swallow him whole? Parker. What he lacked in height he made up for with useless facts and biased opinions. Parker, an engineering graduate of M.I.T. with another Masters in Science, will graciously remind you of that. Parker tends to think that he has the right answer to everything. Excluding his I.Q., Parker does the most with the least, in terms of respect, and manners. Being the oldest sibling meant that he watched his father's rise to independent success and somehow feels entitled to whatever he wants. Parker also remained aware that he was James' only biological child. He used that fact when it benefited his position against his other siblings. Though he was very protective of them both, deep down he felt he should be the one who gets the most from the inheritance and family estate.

Parker believes that 'White Privilege' is a concept created by Black People meant to hold White People back, instead of a system put in place so long ago for that direct reason: to give advantage to few.

Parker thinks that most Black people and minorities are selfish, free-loading scammers and if they don't like how they are being treated in America, they should just go back to their own countries… even if they were BORN IN AMERICA. Often forgetting that his own mother immigrated from Slovakia…

Due to Parker's 'FOKE (Fake Woke) Mindset', he's crippled his growth to learn anything new that doesn't adhere to the beliefs he already holds dear. Parker is basically James West Jr. He talks a lot and thinks he's making sense while using his platform to spread hate and feed into social stereotypes that mistreat people who don't belong to the rich upper class. Parker was once quoted saying, "Disabled people aren't trying hard enough. Disability is simply lazy people trying to get free money. Work harder like my dad."

When you go through life having everything handed to you by the hard work of someone else, seeing other's struggle may not make sense. Furthermore, when you're accustomed to privilege, equality feels like oppression.

Despite Parker, Rebecca, and Broc's shortcomings, there were several people all over the world that agreed with and looked up to them.

Hard to believe that such vile viewpoints were met with praise, but this is America where most of their fans lived. Weekly watching their evil pranks, viral racism, and entitled supremacy was met with even more fans, cheering them on in admiration or envy-which spoke for where the world was during this time. Not everyone was a fan of their antics however.

Several anti-hate groups attempted to shut WSS and MATADOR down, but the two companies proved to be too powerful due to their ties with the FBI, CIA, government, and political candidates. Mr. James West had his hand in everything from entertainment to technology to international relations. One might say, he knew where Osama Bin Laden was hiding before it was revealed to the public where he was found.

Whenever his children went too far with their internet show, his 'clean-up' team would compose a tone deaf apology and resume business as usual. Two of the biggest West scandals involved no other than, 'The Savage', Broc West.

The first involved a Puerto-Rican elementary school student's father whose car battery died on the wrong side of town. Wearing a Hawaiian shirt, flip flops, and cargo shorts, Miguel Miranda approached several parents in the private elementary school parking lot in the Bel Air community in West Los Angeles. He hadn't shaved that day but was eager to get his daughter to her first day of 3rd grade. He wore something fun because Isabel liked when he didn't wear his usual suits.

Miguel was money conscious single father and though he could afford the private school for his daughter, he choose not to spend his money on luxury vehicles. His car was very practical compared to the others in the school parking lot. A Honda that happened to be about 15 years old but still ran good enough most of the time.

"Hey, you wouldn't have any jumper cables would you," Miguel asked a couple. The husband looked Miguel directly in the eyes and refused to respond as the wife entered the passenger seat, desperately avoiding eye contact. Miguel asked 4 other families and people nearby for help and was ignored just the same. As luck would have it, Broc was among those in the parking lot of the school that day. He was passenger to Kim, his personal trainer as she dropped her son off to school. Broc watched Miguel speak to several strangers.
    "What's that dirty looking guy doing over here? Is he begging for money? Jumper cables? Bull shit. He's probably trying to scam anyone he can find. This is Bel Air. He doesn't belong here," Broc said to Kim as they sat in their car watching Miguel's desperation. "Maybe he's actually in some sort of trouble," Kim argued, pulling off in her silver Mercedes Benz. "No. I'm placing a call. He looks suspicious," Broc argued taking out his phone. Broc called the police.

"911, what's your emergency," the operator asked.

"Hi. I'd like to report a disturbance at Bel Air Elementary School. There's a bum hassling people in the parking lot and I think he's armed," Broc said into the phone. Kim raised her eyebrows and whispered, "I don't think I saw anything. He didn't have a gun."

Broc pulled the phone away from his face and whispered back to her, "better safe than sorry. So many assholes shooting up schools these days."

Miguel had to get to work and was eager to get off the private school property. He called roadside assistance as no other parents would acknowledge him outside. Miguel went into the school and explained his situation to the principal.

"Excuse me, sir. My daughter goes to your school. Her name is Isabel Miranda. My car battery died outside and I'm waiting for road side assistance to come. I just wanted to let you know that they would be on property soon. They said it would be about 15 minutes or so." The principal obliged and saw no issue in letting Miguel Miranda wait for assistance. 30 minutes passed and still no sign of road side assistance.

Miguel stood by his car, in the parking lot that was now mostly absent of people but filled with cars. Two squad cars pulled up with their lights on within minutes. Miguel knowing what was about to happened, sighed and threw his head back.

The first police officer exited his car with his hand on his gun, and said, "is there a problem? We had a report of a disturbance in the area about a man that fits your description."

"No. I just dropped my daughter off at school and my car battery died. I'm waiting for AAA right now," Miguel responded. "That's your car right there," the second officer condescendingly asked, pointing to the old green vehicle with rust around the edges closest to the ground.

"Yes, sir," Miguel answered.
"I'm going to need to see some identification," the first officer stated, still with his hand on his gun.

"Are you carrying any weapons we need to know about," the second officer asked, as Miguel handed over his identification.
"No, sir. I told you. I'm here waiting for road side assistance. My daughter is Isabel Miranda and today is her first day of school," Miguel said.

The less aggressive officer went into the school to verify Miguel's story with the principal. Once he came out, the aggressive officer was still harassing Miguel who by now took a glance at his own bare skin and realized the reason for the allegations.

After exchanging words with the officers for several minutes, road side assistance pulled up.

"See, they're here," Miguel said, letting out an annoyed sigh. The officers got back in their vehicles and pulled off.

The second Broc Scandal happened a few months later. During a party in the Hollywood Hills, Broc was among the multitude of celebrity guests. A well known Black entertainer was there as well, who also had a father in power. His name was Skylar Taylor (Sky-T). Skylar and Broc got into an altercation near the pool that Broc instigated by saying, "You wouldn't be here if your dad wasn't who he is, shucking and jiving to entertain us like the fucking clown that he is."

"You're one to talk, white boy. You and your heartless klan member family wouldn't be shit if your dad didn't get lucky with creating that code," Skylar retorted.

"At least my dad has a brand of his own," Broc with his blonde, bouncy hair yelled causing other party goes to watch. The drunken, drug filled party halted to watch the two exchange words.

"Alright. Well at least I know who my real dad is," Skylar jabbed at Broc. Most people knew that Broc was not James' biological son, and used that to get underneath his skin.

Later that night, Broc convinced some of the other party goers that Skylar had stolen some goods from the master bedroom. The police came, took Broc's side, and didn't recognize Skylar from television. But did that matter? Skylar ended up with several guns pulled on him and his friends over a lie. Skylar's crime? Sticking up for himself and telling the officers that he didn't do anything. Skylar's weapon? Having brown skin.

These stories later went viral causing outrage among several people in Hollywood and on social media. Turns out that Miguel Miranda was a small business owner with a lot of lawyers for friends. Broc was seen bragging on social media for calling the police on a bum at Bel-Air Elementary School. Miguel got wind of this and took it to the press.

Broc and Mr. West went on television to apologize to Miguel, Skylar and his famous father for any confusion, arguing that they weren't racist. Mr. West owned a NBA basketball team and occasionally contributed scholarships to fund Black educational programs. This was his defense for his son's actions whenever they found themselves in hot water regarding race.

CHAPTER TWO: GWEILO

Sunday, April 1st. 11:15 p.m.

Let's backtrack a bit, shall we? It was nightfall when they arrived Shanghai. All the stars were closer. The darkest night with the brightest flashes of light. The moon appeared to be placed in the sky like it was plucked from another planet's atmosphere. Though we all look at the same moon at different times, in different places... it didn't look the same.

Following their arrival to Pudong International Airport in Shanghai, the trio found their driver who was holding up a sign that read, "Parker West". The driver was a bald old man with the face of a calm, quiet child. Innocent but wise. Spoke only when spoken to. He was dressed in a charcoal colored suit paired with light blue tennis shoes. It became apparent that he wore the tennis shoes because they made him walk faster. He was a man on his feet, transporting people and their luggage for several hours of the day.

A gentleman, the driver was, offered to carry all of Rebecca's luggage since she was a woman. Rebecca wearing her appropriated Chinese fashion, followed behind, updating her social media accounts to her Asia arrival. Parker and Broc, jet-lagged, were not too far behind.

Once in the vehicle, they began the trek to their hotel via the freeway. Every half mile or so, there was a bright flash coming from the overhead signs above the freeway, directing drivers and their passengers where their exits were.

FLASH. FLASH. FLASH.

The flashes were almost blinding, especially at night. Parker sat in the front seat, using his hand as a visor to the flashes of light, turned to the driver and asked, "Ming, is it? What is that?"

"Oh. Yes. That is our surveillance system. The moment you arrive China, the government takes pictures of you and tracks your every move. We use facial recognition technology to keep everyone safe. If you were to commit a crime here, the system only has to search for your face and find you in less than 7 minutes, " the driver explained.

FLASH. FLASH. FLASH.

The trio arrived their hotel with just enough time to check in and go to bed.

All caught up now? Where were we? Right… Shanghai. High noon. Day 10.

Wednesday, April 11th 12:22 p.m.

In the air of the entire city lived a never ending stench. The smell of spices, vinegar, metallic, and dust made for an aromatic concoction. The smell at times pleasant, quickly passed alluding to whatever reason most of the locals wore medical masks. Pollution perhaps? Or maybe the public hole in the ground found in restrooms instead of a toilet, that you were expected to squat over when it was time to do your business. Whatever the smell was, it made quite the impression.

The trio, Rebecca, Broc, and Parker are walking through Shanghai, a city they've never been to. They were drawn in by the photos and videos of the Oriental Pearl Tower, wanted to see it in person, and perhaps film a couple episodes of WSS in the Chinese city.

Approaching the crosswalk, a small, very old Chinese woman wearing multi-colored, dark, ratted clothing, a bright colorful scarf, and missing all of her teeth, approached them laughing quietly and speaking her foreign language. She looked as if she wanted to say something to them despite knowing that they could not understand what she was saying. She pressed on, almost irritated that they did not respond. Bewildered, Parker waved his hands at her, "Go away, you crazy old bat. We don't understand you." The old woman proceeded to get really close into Parker's face following his remarks.

He could practically taste her bitter breath as she continued rambling in Mandarin Chinese, no longer laughing.

She was serious now. Her eyes tightened and zoomed in on Parker's eyes. The green pedestrian "GO" light was about to turn to "STOP".

That's when she disappeared.

Distracted Parker attempted to cross the street before the crosslight turned red. He did not make it in time. That's when his face immediately popped up on two video screens above the cross walk with a message, "Jaywalkers will be captured using facial recognition technology."

While the trio has traveled a lot of Earth for fun, exploring, and to find new cultures to learn about…this part of China had not been touched. The Chinese culture in Shanghai was unlike any other they'd seen before. The local people of Shanghai stopped to stare if you were different.

If you were Black, some of them even stared with frowns on their faces. The frown was hard to distinguish as to whether it was angry at the Black people for visiting, disgusted, or confused. Either way, it was not welcoming at all. Broc enjoyed his observation with a strong belly-laugh causing a scene.

"It looks like we're not the only ones getting gawked at. Look at that Black chick," Broc pointed as they waited in line for the the Oriental Pearl Tower at The Bund which is a waterfront area in Shanghai. There was a Black, possibly American woman being stared and pointed at by a Chinese family as she stood nearby. She was wearing a 'GUNS N' ROSES' shirt and skinny jeans. Parker began to film some of it while Rebecca attempted to protect their place in line. The Chinese people kept trying to cut them in line…frustrating Rebecca.

"You're not going to FUCKING cut me," Becky scoffed. There were hundreds of people in outside of the building in line waiting to pay. The tower could hold hundreds of people. Another hundred were in line waiting to enter the tower… and several hundred others were lined up inside of the building waiting their turn to begin the extremely sought after tour.

It took several hours to get up to the top of the Tower. By the time they reached the highest point, night had officially come. The observation deck had see through floors in highest capsule (sphere). It was called the Space Capsule. They discretely shot some footage of the Chinese locals and some of the fellow tourists all the way to the top that audio would be added to later.

"Bro, if I had to fuck one of them, I think I would go for that toothless bitch from earlier. She may not be much to look at, but that blow job would be fire," Broc laughed.

"All she needs is a good makeover and some teeth. I know a guy. Actually, Broc, YOU know a guy. That dentist who gave you a few implants after that fight with the Middle Eastern kid. The one whose family owns that restaurant chain in the valley back home," Becky laughed.

"Becky, the point is… never mind. You never gave a good blow job in your life. That's why you can't keep a man," Broc laughed. "Will you both shut the fuck up," Parker paused. "I don't want to picture my little sister giving anyone a blow job, toothless or not," he finished.

It was absolutely breathtaking to see all of Shanghai from the top of the tower. Most cities have a different type of magic to them at night than they do in the day. Santorini, Las Vegas, Paris, Miami,… to name a few. Shanghai was definitely one of them. Some parts of Shanghai looked run down & very poor during the day. Hundreds of brown and tan apartment towers featuring thousands of apartments with clothing hanging from the windows. You would never be able to tell at night due to the fluorescent lights hiding all of the overlooked pits of darkness.

The trio exited the Oriental Pearl Tower and continued their exploration of the city. They were in the heart of the technology district. Though several other buildings were a sight to see, with glowing lights, futuristic architecture, and landscaping, nothing stood out the way OPT did.

It was a struggle to properly direct any taxi to a destination without a room key card featuring the hotel's name in Mandarin, along with a map on the back. Most of the taxi drivers didn't want to deal with any foreigners and would just say, "No," before driving off without them.

"Parker, isn't that the lady that was at the intersection earlier," Becky pointed to an old Chinese lady with her multi-colored attire, staring up into the sky, seemingly unaware of the world around her. "Let's go fuck with her," Parker stated walking her direction.

"Noooo. Leave her alone, guys. Let's go back to the room so we can get on our flight tomorrow," Becky protested as the most 'sensible' one in the trio. "Stop being so sensitive, Becky. Relax," Broc said.

"Maybe we should give her some money or our leftovers after we eat," Becky said. "No. Pfft. She can get a job like the rest of us if she wants money. Money is in exchange for goods or services ONLY. Too many lazy people out there wanting a GOD DAMNED hand out. I work hard for my money. I'm not giving it to some crazy hobo woman on the street," Parker said with an entitled laugh.

Parker and Broc approached the old woman as Becky tip-toed just a few feet behind.

"Hello," the old woman stated in perfect English, a complete

22

180 from earlier. "How can I help you," she calmly asserted. The trio laughed in bewilderment and shock. "Wow, so you speak English? What was all of that earlier," Parker asked.

"I speak many things, Gweilo (foreign devil)," the old woman responded licking her toothless gums and staring at the trio individually but intensely. She smiled like she did before, exposing her pink gums and firm cheekbones.

With a sense of urgency, her staring halted to her words, "Come. Come. Hurry now." The old woman led the trio into a very small shop with no windows at the end of the street in the technology district.

"What the fuck are we doing," whispered Becky, updating her social media accounts again. Hashtag Travel. Hashtag Sky Miles. Hashtag "Wish you were here".

"Bro, this old lady might be trying to rob us. She looks poor," said Broc. "Let's just see what she's showing us," Parker said curiously following close behind the mysterious woman with the colorful head scarf.

Her head scarf appeared to light up whenever the light from The Oriental Pearl Tower reflected nearby, almost as if they were in tune with one another. The similar vibrance intrigued curious Parker.

Convincing his siblings to join his late adventure, the trio entered the shop with annoyed hesitation. Inside of the shop was nothing but textured fabric; colorful blankets, old feathery pillows, and exactly three quilted bean bag chairs.

The trio slumped into each of their bean chairs following the hand motion of the old woman to, "please sit."

"I am Zingaro. But you can call me Zinga. God calls me Z," Zinga chuckled.

"Isn't Zingaro Italian, and aren't you Chinese," Parker asked, humbly boasting his cultural knowledge.

Zinga looks down at her skin and pulls out a small mirror. "Oh. Hmm. I guess I am Chinese," she says as if she forgot.

She then clears her throat incessantly for several minutes. Awkward silence surrounded the room.

"Okay, and... what do you want from us," Becky stated with impatience. "I want to give you something," Zinga responded.
"I think we're good. We have enough blankets," Broc laughed, looking around.

"I want to give you something special. A souvenir. Something you can use for a lifetime," Zinga said, touching each of their hands with her nails, softly.

"Dude, I'm really not in the mood for any freaky shit. If she's offering blow jobs, I'm out," Broc whispered to Parker who sat at the edge of his bean chair, irrevocably intrigued.

"Let's just see what this is about, bro. Calm down," Parker responded.

"How much," Parker stated.

"Blow jobs? Oh that's extra. But I'm not doing that today," Zinga toothlessly smiled, embarrassing them that she heard their crass whispers.

"How did you..." Broc began.
"I speak many things, remember Gweilo," Zinga said plainly.

"Now. I need your passports and the rest of your yuan. You're leaving tomorrow, no," Zinga said, fidgeting with something in her lap.

"The rest of our money? And our passports? What if we only have 200 yuan left between all of us," Parker asked looking around the cozy yet uncomfortable room.

"It doesn't matter how much you have. You will see. But I need it all and your passports just temporarily," Zinga responded circling the candlelit room.

Zinga took each of their passports and stared at them intently, gently rubbing her hand over the faces in the photos of the worn out passports.

"Parker, if she steals our identity and ends up buying a yacht in Miami, I'm going to hang you by the balls," Broc whispered, uncaring if she heard him this time.

Each of them piled up their remaining coins in hopes of a memorable magic trick from Zinga. "Close your eyes, Gweilos… er, I mean, darlings," Zinga said with a softening snap and toothless grin.

"Why," Becky asked suspiciously, giving Zinga a dirty look.

"Because I'm going to give you something priceless," Zinga responded.

"See, I knew it. Soon as we close our eyes, we're getting robbed of our kidneys," Broc whispered, adjusting his body to leave.

"I'm going to tell each of you your fortune and grant a wish that you have," Zinga whispered, looking directly at Broc, who was scanning the room with judgement in his eyes.

"Alright. I wanna play," Becky said, loosening up.

Becky took her phone out to snap a photo of Zinga and the colorful but dim surroundings.

"NO PHONES. NO PICTURES. NO VIDEO," Zinga said

sternly.

"Sorry," Becky said, putting her phone away as Broc sneaked a picture anyway.

Zinga grabbed Becky's hands and carefully examined them while looking into her eyes. Becky had a hard time maintaining eye contact with the intense old woman. She had a hard time maintaining eye contact with anyone unless she had their dick in her mouth.

"Ah. Ha! I see," Zinga exclaimed, looking straight through Becky.

"You see what," Becky said, unenthusiastically.

"I see you. I see you beyond this costume that you wear," Zinga said simply.

"I'm not wearing a costume," Becky stated.

"But you are. We are all wearing a costume from time to time. Some of us get to take them off. Some of us wear them to keep the world out. Some of us wear them... to change who we think we are. And others apply costumes forever. Which one are you," Zinga said, tilting her head back to back following Becky's inconsistent eye contact.

Zinga placed a bright red coin into Becky's palm, grasped her fingers, and closed them over the coin. The coin had a golden glow to it in the right light and there were raised Chinese letters on it with a hole in the middle.

Zinga then proceeded to Broc, giving him the same treatment, grabbing his hands to examine and look into his blue ocean eyes.

After looking into Broc's eyes for several moments, Zinga's eyes widened and she stood back startled. A visible chill ran over her as if she saw a ghost.

26

"What," Broc eagerly asked, noticing Zinga's change.

"You're the king. Or at least you think you are. You treat everyone else like they are beneath you, often putting others in danger because of your closed minded beliefs. Ha! We all shit under the same moon... for now. We will be buried or burned and blown into the sea with each other for all of eternity. You treat people badly because you are afraid that you are indeed shit. You are right. You are no King... You are shit," Zinga began.

"King? Shit? What the fuck are you talking about," Broc said with agitation. Broc began to get up and snatched his sweaty hands away from Zinga, slightly knocking Parker down in his spoiled, childlike fury.

"Don't you want your coin," Zinga asked staring at the shimmering red coin in her hand.

"No. I don't want shit you have to offer, shit lady," Broc said, tossing some of Zinga's fabrics around near the door.

"Okay. As you wish," Zinga said, with a satisfied grin.

"I still want to try... let's see if you can read me," Parker smiled, eager to have some fun, leaning even closer in towards Zinga and her sour breath.

As with the others, Zinga grabbed Parker's small hands and looked into his eyes. This time she began shaking her head as if to scold a small child. Zinga began to draw something into Parker's left hand with her fingers only.

"Big little man, you are wise. But only a fool thinks that he knows everything. You should listen to other's stories and learn from them. Listen more. Speak less. No greater teacher than life," Zinga smiled at Parker.

Zinga placed a coin in Parker's hand.

"Put this under your pillow tonight and a wish will be granted," Zinga said, scanning the room at all three of them.

"Thanks. I guess," Parker said, placing his weathered passport back into his suit jacket.

"Are you idiots done now? Can we get out of this shit hole," Broc asked, throwing his long blonde hair over his shoulder as he still stood at the door.

Becky and Parker faced Broc and then looked back towards the kaleidoscope framed room where Zinga was once sitting.

"Where did she go," Parker asked.

"Fuck, I don't know. Probably to catch and cook a poodle or something," Broc said, rolling his eyes.

"Well you were facing the direction she was sitting. So ... did you see her leave," Parker asked, confused. Becky turned her iPhone flashlight on and started searching the small shop for doors or other exits. There were none.

The trio looked underneath the fluffy pillows, blankets, and furry walls for a sign of Zinga. Her colorful scarf subtly shined while laying in the spot where she once sat.

"Old lady? Zinga? Cool disappearing trick. But we're going to go. You can come out and say bye... or keep hiding, but we're out," Parker said, while walking toward the exit.

"Let's get out of here. It doesn't matter," Becky said, twirling her souvenir red coin between her sparkly fake nails.

The trio exited the small abandoned shop, consistently looking back to see if Zinga would appear in the darkness. The further away that they got, the Oriental Pearl Tower lit up like purple magic, guiding their way back to the hotel.

CHAPTER THREE: BROKEN MIRROR

Thursday, April 12th 8:08 a.m.

Morning came quickly. The trio shared a large lavish suite with individual bedrooms at a luxury hotel called The Grand Kempinski. The hotel featured a breathtaking view of the Shanghai skyline and Huangpu River that could be observed in the day or the night. No words can describe the detail put into making this hotel what it is.

The most expensive hotel in all of Shanghai. Italian marbled counter tops, marveled floors, doubly vanity mirrors, oversized bathrooms, whirlpool tubs, ceiling to floor windows, and amenities fit for a sorcerer. Their suite was designed in Luxury Art Deco furniture with many chandeliers.

The Grand Kempinski was place where if you had enough money, you would be treated like a king. In Chinese culture, it is not customary to tip. Some even see it as insulting to be tipped for their services. As if they are not paid a decent wage?

However, every once in a while, a business minded bell-boy took advantage of the naive tourists by rubbing his thumb and index finger together. Needless to say, when they took advantage of unsuspecting tourists who were already prepared to pay such a high price tag for a room, they came out well ahead.

There was a loud knock at the door of the suite. "One moment. I'm coming," Broc stated, laying on the royal blue, velvet couch, half asleep. Broc rubbed his eyes and approached the door. The knock began again as Broc opened the door.

"Yes," Broc asked, rubbing the boogers out of his eyes.

"I have the dry cleaning for this room," the hotel attendant whispered with a goofy look on his face. "Okay, cool. Thanks," Broc said, about to shut the door. The attendant rubbed his fingers together to ask for a tip. "Mayo," Broc said, shaking his head "No."

Broc laughed and shut the door in the attendant's face.

Once Broc shut the door, he instantly noticed something different. His eyes scanned from the decorative double doors to his hand to his arms... and he screamed. He took his other hand to his arm to touch his bare skin. Broc then faced the round, golden, decorative mirror on the wall beside the entryway.

He wanted to call out for help but knew that what he saw would not send others to his aid.

Broc could not believe his eyes. Staring into his reflection, his eyes remained the same, mostly. They were no longer blue but still just as intense. His face shape had not been altered much. His hair texture was kinky, curly, and appeared to be growing about 11 inches towards the sun... instead of 22 inches towards the ground as it was before.

His skin was a deep brown with hints of gold. His blue eyes were now dark brown. Cheekbones became chiseled and defined. Broc became what he envied and hated. Broc was a black man now.

He immediately went to Parker's room to wake him, but stopped remembering that he now would not be recognizable.

He needed a plan so that he wouldn't startle his older brother. A plan so that his brother wouldn't see a black man in their suite and instinctively attack him. He went to his untouched bed and grabbed a white bedspread and threw it over his entire body.

Broc revisited his steps one last time, hoping not to accidentally wake his sister in the process. Broc looked into Rebecca's room and she was still sound asleep with a bottle of wine at her bedside.

"Parker, bro. Wake up," Broc whispered to his brother. "Broc, it's early. Give me 10 more minutes," Parker grunted.

"NO. I NEED YOU UP NOW," Broc demanded, realizing his voice had also changed. "Why are you hiding under that blanket? And why are you talking like that," Parker whispered, turning back into his pillow.

"Something happened and I need you to remain calm, okay? Fucking... Don't fucking hit me, man. I mean it. Don't scream. That old bitch. Zinga or whatever,...." Broc began before Parker interrupted.

"You had a nightmare about Zinga and you want me to hold you. Not now. Turn my light off please," Parker said still facing the opposite direction.

Broc let out a deep loud sigh.

"Look, I'm going to take the blanket off of me, but I need you to promise that you won't hurt me. Zinga put a spell on me last night. I found the coin that I threw back at her yesterday night in my room. It was on the nightstand. I didn't even take it," Broc whispered sternly.

"Okay. And? What are you saying," Parker asked.

"Fuck it. Here goes," Broc said dropping the blanket.

"AH!" Parker exclaimed.

"You promised not to scream," Broc said.

"I didn't promise you shit. Who the fuck are you," Parker asked, sliding out of bed onto the floor. "Here. Take my wallet. You can have my wallet," Parker said reaching for his wallet.

Parker hopped onto his feet and took an aggressive stance towards the unfamiliar face and body, preparing to fight or defend himself.

"PARKER XAVIER WEST, IT'S ME. IT'S BROC. IT'S ME, DUDE. ZINGA DID THIS," Broc explained, feeling defeated and starting to cry hysterically.

Parker zoomed in on Broc's familiar eyes which remained unchanged other than color.

"Broc? Sweet Fucking Jesus. What the fucking fuck! How is this even possible?! Dude, I gotta get my camera," Parker began reaching for his camera equipment.

"No," Broc said through his teeth. "Dude this is sick, we have to film it. You look amazing. This is better than that Halloween you went in blackface as a Black Panther. Your hair. Is that a wig? FUCK YES," Parker insisted reaching to pull Broc's hair. Broc knocked the camera out of Parker's hands. Less than a second later a scream emerged from Rebecca's room.

"My tits! Oh my GOD! They're deflated. Oh no. Oh no. Oh no," Becky screamed.

The boys ran to Becky's room and saw her curvy shadow feeling around in the dark at her flattened chest. Becky assumed her most recent boob job was simply botched. Broc turned the light on and Becky screamed again. "Who's the black dude, Parker. Your new token Black friend, " Becky asked, annoyed.

"Nope, your new token Black brother, you shallow bitch. Go look in the mirror," Black Broc said, calmly.

"What? What do you mean? What's going on? What's wrong with my face," Becky frantically said, feeling her face as she stumbled out of her bed with white sheets wrapped around her ankles.

Approaching the bathroom, she continued to stumble, afraid of what she may see, while simultaneously attempting to process the rude, Black man who stood in her room accompanied by her older brother.

The light switch came on and in the reflection was the melted remains of a former beauty pageant prom queen who had so much plastic surgery that Michael Jackson could judge her. One eye seemed to remain in tact as the left one drooped towards the running mascara it sat lazily above. As if it were a really bad dream, Rebecca slowly ran her once slender hands down her face seeing her fingers were no longer capable of hand modeling. Her fingers now looked like she had been dragging them across motor oil and concrete for the passed 45 years.

Her veneers were no longer present. Instead her teeth were yellow, cracked, and filled with spaces. The teeth of a devoted meth addicted prostitute that knocked a few out to give better oral sex. Rebecca traced the brown deposits across her once pearl teeth and screamed again. As she screamed, the scene ran in slow motion. Rebecca slid everything off the counter as her cosmetics and perfumes crashed onto the marble floor beneath. Broken glass went everywhere.

Another howl emerged from Ruined Rebecca's lips as she grabbed a piece of the shattered glass and took it to her wrist. Black Broc and Poised Parker ran over to her, forcing her hand to drop the glass.

"Ew. Don't fucking touch me," Rebecca scoffed, shrugging Broc off of her in one quick motion.

"Becky, it's me. Will you cut the shit and pull it together. We need to focus so we can figure this out and reverse whatever spell that old gypsy put on us last night," Broc responds in an authoritative tone.

Becky touches her mangled face and screams again. Parker goes to her bedside and grabs a prescription bottle of Xanax for her to calm down. In what seemed like a familiar ritual, Becky grabs the bottle, takes a pill and chases it with the bottle of wine at her bedside.

Becky sighs and says, "give me a few minutes. I need this to kick in or maybe I'll die by then."

"We don't have a few minutes. We need to find that woman and fix this. Our flight leaves in a few hours," Parker says heading towards his dark room to grab his things.

"We'll get you one of those medical masks that all the Asians wear and a curly brown wig. You'll be fine," Parker reassures her.

"What about me? What can you do to help me," Broc asks, rubbing his skin vigorously.

"Well, you're Black. I don't know. There's no helping that," Parker responds, plainly.

"Fuck you, man," Broc whispers.

"Listen. I'm not trying to be a dick. But looks like I'm the only one that can help you two. Nothing happened to me, so…I'm good," Parker says confidently.

"Can't we just call dad," Broc asks.

"You really think Mr. James 'Atheist' West is going to believe any of this shit. He doesn't believe in anything but money. And that's what he's going to think we want if we contact him. Money can't fix this," Parker responds, using several hand gestures to spell out his point like he always does.

"I can bleach my skin or something? Maybe shave or straighten my hair," Broc says. The look of a lost child surrounded by strangers washes over Broc's face. Becky finally realizes this IS her little brother.

"I can go see Dr. Rosenburg in Beverly Hills. He can fix anything. He'll help me," Becky whines, carefully touching her face as if it were wounded.

"Sure, you guys. Do all those things. But if this woman was able to do this to you without physically being present, do you think physically enduring some type of aesthetic procedure will permanently change anything back to normal for good," Parker reasoned, using his hands again.

"I don't know. Maybe," Becky says crying, while staring at her new Black brother.

CHAPTER FOUR: THE MULETA OBSCURES THE SWORD

11:00 a.m.

The trio departed the hotel to head back to the abandoned shop they adventured to the night before. Becky wore a bedazzled surgeon mask from the gift store and a headscarf to cover the bald spots & ratted areas where her luxurious brown curls once were. Broc was just Black. There was nothing he could do to hide that. Parker feeling fortunate to not have succumbed to any spells, wore a smile as he led the pack of three.

An unlikely trio they were as they walked together through Pudong Shanghai. The stares and whispers from the day prior had intensified and made them all uncomfortable. Even Parker, who was not suffering from any drastic physical alteration was receiving the stares of association. Guilty by association. He was escorting a Black man and an extremely disfigured woman down a well lit street. In the eyes of onlookers you could see worry, wonder, and disgust.

Becky's once strong, manicured posture was drooped over. She no longer had large breasts to push out for the world to see so she caved into herself and slumped while she walked.

Broc's confident posture remained mostly, but he was on guard as he was covered in something that could not be hidden. The largest organ on his body- skin. Something that where he was from was the target of unwarranted violence, aggression, and hatred. He felt like there was a surveillance team following his every move at all times. With the camera surveillance software that surrounded the city, he literally was already being watched and recorded.

36

And though Broc appeared to be tall and strong on the outside, inside he felt powerless against others' false perceptions of who he actually was.

"We're here," Parker stated as they approached Zinga's shop. It was still dark and abandoned. There was a sign on the door that read, "OUT TO LUNCH. BACK MONDAY." The trio peered through the dirty windows to see if anyone was present.

Broc reached in his pocket and handed Parker his crisp brand new passport. "I'm not going anywhere looking like this," Broc says. "You? What about me? Look at me! I'm more fucked up than you are. You just are going to get hassled by cops now. Big deal," Butchered Becky scoffs.

A few feet away there was a small, very thin Chinese boy observing the trio. He was wearing what looked like it used to be a school uniform, a wrinkled white shirt and navy blue pants. The boy walked over to them, handed them a small piece of paper and a bullfighting brochure with a Matador and a bull featured prominently on the front. "What is this," Parker asked the small boy. "No English," the boy said, pointing to the shop and back to the group of Americans.

The trio huddled around each other to read the note. The note read: "Zinga says, find a way to Spain. The city of Seville. Meet Mister Sebastian Barrio at Plaza de Torros de Sevilla."

5 minutes later. 11:32 a.m.

Suddenly the little Chinese boy appeared again, and pulled something out of the front of his pants.

It looked as if he had the envelope in his underwear all day. He handed a damp, manila envelope to Black Broc. Inside of the envelope was a plane ticket, a passport with his new face on it, and the words, "Go alone or you'll never come back."

The young boy vanished.

Parker carefully dissected the bullfighting brochure as Broc examined the authenticity of his new passport.

"Trippy," Broc whispered.

"Not as trippy as your actual face, bro," Parker laughed.

"I'm hungry," Becky whined facing Chinese locals who walked by nearby with food in their hands.

"Cool. Let's go eat before Broc heads to Spain," Parker says, as he begins shooing away people who were staring too closely at his siblings.

"Get outta here, chinks," Parker scoffs to those judging his family.

"Naw, man. I'll just go at it alone. I'll eat later. I don't really ..." Broc began, observing the laughter and stares directed at him from the locals.
"You don't what? Don't feel like being in public with your face," Becky interrupted.

"Yeah, man. I don't like the looks. It's all making me feel really weird and tired. I just wanna chill and do room service or something," Broc finished with a shrug.

"We're in this together. So let's grab something on the way back to the hotel and get you to the airport, nigger," Parker laughed.

Broc pushed Parker really hard, knocking him into passersby.

"Guys, stop it! I'm sick of it all. Geez," Becky screamed.

"Alright. Alright. Just having some fun," Parker says, still mostly unfazed as he is still the same Parker.

"Well, knock it off. I'm not in the mood," Broc says, adjusting his shirt.

"Is there a problem over here," an English speaking man says maintaining his focus on Black Broc.

"No, we're good," Parker asserts, understanding that his brother's playful actions look different in his new 'Earth-suit'.

The English man leaves the situation and goes back to wherever he came from.

12:15 p.m.

Back at the room, the trio began to google the pamphlet they were given along with the address of Broc's upcoming destination.

"What does bullfighting have to do with any of this," Broc asks staring at Parker who is doing most of the typing.

"I don't know. Maybe that's just the guy that can reverse the spell. Maybe he's a bullfighter? Or maybe he works there? Barrio? Mister Barrio," Parker says, calmly while sipping a cup of hot coffee.

"I cannot seem to find anyone by that name she gave me listed anywhere in Spain. That's weird. Sebastian Barrio seems common enough. You would think there would be at least one on google to find," Parker asserts, squinting his eyes to the bright computer screen.

"Hey guys, maybe she has a bone to pick with dad. I mean... Dad's logo IS a bullfighter," Becky says, while twirling what's left of her stringy hair.

"No. Becky. You don't know anything. I think it's just a coincidence," Parker responds.

"Don't be rude, Parker. You don't know everything, you know. Remember what Zinga said to you last night. Only a fool thinks he knows everything," Rebecca whispered, mocking & rolling her eyes...or what was left of them anyway.

"Yeah, yeah, whatever. HEY YOU GUYSSS! Shut up, Sloth," Parker mocked her in return, still typing away.

"Maybe she has a point. It does make sense, in a way, Parker. Matador and she's sending me to meet someone at a bullfighting ring. Maybe dad killed her brother or something," Broc says.

"Dad doesn't kill people, idiot," Parker says, matter of factly, using hand gestures again.

"But the people he associates with DO KILL PEOPLE," Broc reminds him, mocking his hand gestures.

Parker starts to stare intensely at his new Black brother, in awe of the way the sunlight is hitting his skin.

"You're actually kind of beautiful, little brother. This is a good look for you. It's starting to grow on me," Parker says, eyes widened and eye brows arched.

"Going there alone could be dangerous. I want you to be safe," Parker finishes, still typing into the keyboard.

"What do you suggest? Her note says I have to go alone if I want to return. And it would seem as if this wicked bitch means exactly what she says," Broc reminds him, gazing at the Oriental Pearl Tower outside the window.

"Nah. I'm going with you. Fuck her note," Parker says, shutting the laptop on the marble countertop. Parker begins to stand to his feet and falls onto the floor, face first.

"I can't stand up. I CAN'T FEEL MY LEGS. MY DICK! I CAN'T FEEL MY DICK," Parker says as each of his words gain more volume than the last.

Broc towering over him picks Parker up, drags him from the bar area to the couch, and props him up. He begins to do tests with

40

his legs and arms to see what he can feel and what he cannot feel.

"Can you feel this," Broc asks, applying consistent pressure to every area of Parker's lower body. Broc wanting to prove that this is the work of Zinga then punches Parker in the penis. Parker screams but feels nothing.

"Dude, what the fuck did you do that for," Parker yells. "Did it hurt," Broc asks. "No, but it scared me," Parker responds. "Oh. Good," Broc says, smiling.

"No, not good. I cannot fucking walk now. I need to come with you to help you. Your flight leaves in 5 hours," Parker asserts as Broc props him back up again. Parker scoots to the floor and begins dragging his lifeless legs across the carpet towards the bathroom.

"I have to pee," Parker says. "How do you know you have to pee if you can't feel your dick," Broc asks. "Because I can still feel my bladder and it's full of fucking coffee. I've been drinking coffee all day," Parker responds, nodding to the several empty cups along the bar countertop.

Parker pulls out his limp penis, aims it towards the toilet as dark yellow urine pours from his pink penis onto the bathroom floor.

"Well done, Picasso. I could have helped you," Broc says, face palming.

"I don't want any help," Parker scoffs, unable to scoot himself back into his designer pants. "Moody, aren't we now? Someone or something is going to have to help you, Parker. And it's probably going to be Becky, so you better be nice to her while I'm gone," Broc says, gazing at the Oriental Pearl Tower outside of the floor length window.

Rebecca overhears her name and comes into the room to observe half-naked Parker on his bathroom floor, next to a small puddle. "Nice," Becky laughs with a snort.

"Looks like Zinga doesn't want you to go anywhere," Becky says, pushing food into her deformed mouth. "Keep pushing that food into your mouth and shut it," Parker says scooting his uncooperative body back into the living room area.

"Oh yeah? Well looks like the only thing of yours that you can run now IS your mouth. So there's that," Becky retorts.

"You two. Fuck off. Shut up. If we keep arguing we're never going to reverse this shit. Do you all want to stay this way? You have to get along while I'm gone. I can't worry about this while I'm in Spain," Broc stammers like an angry father whose children didn't wash the dishes after he had been at work all day.

Due to the added circumstance, the roles reverse. Broc becomes the authoritative one. Parker becomes the one told what to do. Parker feeling helpless and childlike is angry at his condition. A condition that he thought he avoided by being somewhat nice to Zinga. Apparently his disingenuous interest in her didn't matter at all.

CHAPTER FIVE: CUSTOMS

1:32 p.m.

Broc arrived the airport just in time to get through Chinese customs and make his 16 hour flight to Seville, Spain. The Delta terminal didn't open until 4pm so Broc was stuck sitting there for a long while. Several Chinese people thought he was a basketball player and asked to take photos with him as he stood awaiting departure.

He kindly obliged as it was a nice break from how he had been treated in the heart of Shanghai. There still were several people that stared with disgust, but it was welcoming to be treated like a star or celebrity. One family in particular made Broc feel uncomfortable. Following the mini-photoshoot with all 7 of them, the eldest lady of the group smiled and was doing her best to communicate for permission to touch his skin and hair. Her shirt had English words on it and Chinese writing. You could tell she didn't know what it said for sure in English, but perhaps it was correct in her native language.

In English her shirt read, "The Pig Is Full Of Many Cats".

Still reaching for Broc's hair, the eager woman shook her head as if to ask, "Yes, can I," while reaching for his bare skin and exposed arms. He furrowed his eyebrows, confused as to what they expected to happen by touching his brown skin. Did they expect it to rub off? Change color? Magically disappear? He hoped so, at least.

One of the woman's smaller children, motioned with her hands for Broc to bend down to her. She wanted to touch his hair too. After one touched his hair, several others ran up to do the same. They laughed in glee and took more photos of each other with the spectacle of the person they saw before them. Year 2018 but it was as if they had never seen a black person before.

Broc began feeling like a zoo exhibit so he backed away and went to hide in the restroom for a little while.

While in the restroom, he did some research on the internet in his phone. He was curious as to what the relationship with the Chinese was with Black people. Were they more disgusted or fascinated with Black people? Broc found that in Hong Kong there was recently a museum exhibit which featured a comparison of Black people to monkeys, apes, and monsters. Many of the Chinese had indeed never seen many Black people before. The racism and beliefs were passed onto their children. The children more likely to point and laugh at these people who have been perceived to be walking and talking animals.

To some of the Chinese people Black people were just that, walking, talking animals. Broc found an article that stated that, "White is not considered a color. But black is a color." Several videos show the Chinese people making fun of Black and African people by applying Black face and fake buttocks to alter their looks. He found references to Sarah Baartman (Saartje Bartman), an African woman from the 1800's who was objectified as a freak show in Europe due to her large buttocks. Still scanning through photos of people in Black face, mimicking Black and African people, Broc felt heavy.

Some of the enhancements reminded Broc of things that his sister had done to change her looks. Was Becky attempting to look Black, without actually having to be Black? The Black features that were praised when had by those of other cultures, but belittled when had by those of Black or African descent.

The deeper that Broc went into the inter-webs, the more hatred he found from other cultures against the Black race. He started to feel like a prisoner in his own skin.

Several ads showing other cultures using skin lightening

creams and potions to make their skin lighter because some believe that lighter skin represented racial superiority, wealth, and power. Many people in Asia were obsessed with having white skin.

Broc became angry and sad at the same time, making a fist with his hand. He started to reflect on his time in Shanghai and the things he observed while his skin was beige versus now that his skin is brown. Some shame creeped into his psyche realizing some of the things that he had done to people who were different than him, specifically Black people.

While many other ethnicities have darker toned people in them, Black people were genetically the furthest away from those who were Caucasian. Other races with darker skin, still had straight hair for instance. Most Black people have kinky, curly, or textured hair... which has become stigmatized as unkempt or unprofessional.

"Fuck," Broc whispered, rubbing the skin on his arm the way that the family had a few moments ago. The deep chocolate complexion of his was not going anywhere. Broc took a deep breath and placed his phone back into his pocket. There was a daydreaming pause.

Broc pulled his phone back out of his pocket and decided to place a phone call on his way to the gate.

"Hello, may I be connected to Sky-T. Um, Skylar Taylor please," Broc asked, hearing a young woman's voice on the other end.

"This is Skylar," Skylar says as he grabs the phone from his girlfriend.

"Yo, this is Broc West,"... Broc began, walking towards his gate with a camouflage backpack over his shoulders.
"What the fuck do you want, Broc? Why are you changing your voice to sound like that? You mocking me," Skylar says.

"No... I. I have a cold. Look, I wanted to apologize to you for some things I have said and done to you in the past. I'm..I'm sorry," Broc said, embarrassed.

"Forget it. Don't worry about it, man. I'm used to it," Skylar says.

"You're used to it? That's awful. No one should be treated the way that I have treated you. We grew up together and honestly I think I've just been jealous of you. You always were better at everything than I was. You had the hottest girls after you," Broc said, holding his head down while ducking from the Chinese family that saw him earlier.

"Jealous of me? Why? Your dad is one of the richest men in the world," Skylar responded.
"Money ain't everything, bro. And it can't buy or fix everything either. Some things just are. There's more important things. People are getting killed for looking different and it's not fair," Broc says, settling into a seat far away from others.

"Dude, where are you? You at some peace retreat or something," Skylar laughs into the phone.

"No. I'm just realizing how shitty of a person I've been most of my life because of who my father is and the color of my skin. It's a stupid reason to think I'm better than everyone else," Broc responded.

"Yeah... of course it is. Tell that to most of America and the rest of the world. Anyway, are you okay, man," Skylar asks, feeling uneasy at Broc's sudden change of heart.

"I'm going through some personal things but I think I'll be alright. Take care," Broc says before hanging up.
Broc calls Skylar back right after hanging up and asks, "Hey. I have another question. What do you use on your hair? You know, to keep it curly, healthy, and moisturized?"

"Shea butter and natural oils," Skylar responds.

"Thanks, man." Broc finishes. Broc was having difficulty maintaining his new hair texture as it was nothing like his once flowing straight locks. He smiled at the new information and proceeded onward.

5 p.m.

Broc makes his way to the gate in time to board the plane. The first stop on the way to Seville is in Zurich, Switzerland.

"I hope they like Black people there," Broc whispers to himself, while looking at his boarding pass.

Aboard the flight there was a flirty flight attendant who looked at Broc how he had yet to be looked at like in his new Earth Suit. He observed from a distance as she spoke perfect Mandarin, Spanish, and English.

Intrigued, Broc followed her with his eyes and occasionally with his entire head. Whenever his head turned however, he could not be discrete. His big curly afro gave him away whenever as he tried to be subtle. He hadn't mastered the art of subtlety yet.

"You doing alright," the large breasted, flight attendant asked Broc while coming down his aisle mid-flight. Her name tag read 'Valentina'.

"Yes, I'm peanuts. I mean, I'm alright. How. How are you," Broc stumbled over his words. The brown skinned beauty responded with a laugh, noticing that he was into her. "I am great. It's going to be an amazing flight. Please let me know if you need anything. I'm Valentina," Valentina responded, touching his shoulder.

Broc felt the blood rush through his entire body and congregate at the tip of his penis when she touched him. Puberty was beginning all over again for him with this new body he had yet to master. He was starting to enjoy it. He enjoyed it so much that he went to the restroom to join 'the mile high club' by himself with thoughts of the golden brown flight attendant whose eyes shined like diamonds.

Upon unbuckling his pants to find his erection, Broc was delightfully surprised that his erect penis was 3 inches longer than the one he previously had.

"Are you fucking kidding me," Broc whispered, laughing.

As he began to delicately and vigorously explore his new body, he closed his eyes and imagined himself with Valentina. Vigorously, he stroked his hand up and down his new penis, amazed at how new the sensations felt. Faster. Faster. FASTER. Griping the shaft with a hold that loosened each time he reached the sensitive head of his dick... he exploded so intensely that he saw stars and was blinded for a moment when the waves of his orgasm came spilling onto his hand, buckling his knees as he stood. Almost falling over, the creamy white substance shot pass Broc's hand and onto the airplane lavatory mirror. Avoiding his own reflection, Broc quickly washed the mirror off with a tissue and washed his hands. With his penis still erect, Broc shoved it in his pants, allowing it to rest on his stomach, hidden by his shirt.

4.5 minutes later, Broc was back in his seat.

Shanghai, 10:14 p.m.

Parker and Rebecca were barely getting along. Parker was the eldest & used to taking care of everyone else. His pride was getting in the way of letting himself be cared for. And Rebecca, though sensitive, could be a bitch when things weren't going her way. The state of her current affairs as in her face, had her in the PMS of all moods. She had no time for Parker's condescending insults and didn't deserve them as she was his caretaker until Broc's return, a spell reversal, or a miracle.

48

"Parker, you need to eat something. What would you like me to order for you. The kitchen is going to close soon," Rebecca asked. "For the 30th time, I'm fine. I'll eat when I get my legs back," Paralyzed Parker stated. "You actually have your legs...soooo," Becky began. "So, I'll eat when I can use them, okay? Is that okay with you," Parker asked.

"It's fine with me. But I think mom and dad would much rather you alive. Can we just call them, please," Becky asked. "And prove to them that we can't handle anything? Absolutely NOT. James would love that too much," Parker responded.

"Such the angry little man, aren't you," Becky whispered, walking away.

A few hours later, Becky discretely called to check on her parents. It was 7am the previous day, back in LA. Lucy, her mother answered. "Hello, darling. How's your trip? Where are my boys," Lucy asked.

"They're fine. I just... I wanted to hear your voice," Becky stated with a deep sigh.

"You sound a little muffled, dear. Are you eating something into the phone. Remember etiquette class,..." Lucy insisted.

Becky's facial deformity was causing her to speak with a lisp and she had cotton in her mouth to prevent the incessant drooling. Her face was getting worse as time went on, not better.

"Alright, mom. Where's dad," Becky asked. "He's off with one of those politician friends of his playing golf. Oh dear, I cannot seem to remember his name. Charles. Cheech... Um.. I don't know," Lucy says. "No worries, mommy," Becky says. "Oh Rebecca, I have to go. The new puppy has got into something again. Bye honey. Send the boys my love. See you soon," Lucy concluded, ending the phone call abruptly.

"Bye, ma-" Becky began realizing the call had already been

disconnected.

Becky went to check on Parker who was laying in his own urine in the middle of his floor. "Just giving up already, huh? It's day one," Becky stated with disappointment. Parker may have smelled like Skid Row in Los Angeles but he was busy on the internet researching information about gypsies, spells, and curses.

Disgusted, and holding her nose, Becky asked, "Can I call housekeeping to run you a bath and clean this mess up?"

"Turns out that Zinga's full name "Zingaro" translates to 'Gypsy' in Italian," Parker says to Becky as he takes notes on the hotel notepad. "Oh, cool," Becky responds sarcastically in a failed attempt to roll her eyes.

"There's also an instance of something similar to this happening in Barcelona 100 years ago. Happened in America about 155 years ago, right before slavery ended. A group of slave owners were raping their slaves and the offspring of those relationships with the slaves. Sneaking into their homes on the plantations in the middle of the night, these men were taking negro slave wives away from their husbands to fuck them in the shed or wherever their wives wouldn't catch them with the negro slave women. Their story is later told by the grandchildren of their forefathers passing down these stories of owning slaves in previous generations. Turns out the slave owners become slaves after a chance meeting with a traveling magician that promised them a fortune beyond their wildest dreams. They say they woke up in a different body, a negro woman body. Look here," Parker pointed to some articles on his laptop screen that he was researching.

"The negro woman or former slave owner was sold and sold again. She was getting raped repeatedly and kept insisting that she was not a nigger. She screamed this every time she was raped. She said her name was Robert Ruffin Barrow, one of the wealthiest plantation owners in the South who had recently gone missing. My name is Robert Ruffin Barrow and I am no negro. I am no slave. I am no nigger," Parker read aloud.

"Ooh. Ooh. Here's another. A group of the people working with Hitler to banish all those that did not meet his criteria woke up and were heard screaming that they were not Jews. They claimed that they woke up that way. He killed them anyway," Parker read, getting morbidly excited about history.

"What does any of this shit have to do with us? We don't have any slaves," Becky says. "True. But we do have an ungodly amount of followers and viewers that subscribe to our belief systems. We influence those people, especially those looking for something to believe in, look up to, or be entertained by," Parker asserted, sipping coffee.

"Are you saying what we do is wrong," Becky asked. "I'm not saying it's wrong or right. But it is something that we do. And we have got a lot of backlash from the content that we put out there. I don't know. I'm just doing a lot of reading and wondering if we were targeted in some way. Maybe it wasn't James (Dad) after all. But something to do with Matador, that I'm not putting my finger on completely. Broc may be in danger," Parker concludes with an escalated speech.

In the Sky, Friday, April 13th 12:00 a.m.

Broc had finally stopped molesting himself in the port-a-potty in the clouds. He was in the 8th of his 14 hours in the air towards Zurich where he would connect to his flight to Spain. Valentina had come by several times to tend to her guests. She spent some extra time with Broc and he learned that she lives in Barcelona. Valentina would be connecting to her flight home after going to Zurich.

"Yeah, so Barcelona is a 2 hour flight from Seville. Maybe you could come visit me sometime if you're going to be there a while," Valentina concluded, discretely slipping Broc her phone number along with his peanuts.

"I'd love to do you. I mean, do that. I'd love to do that. See you. I.. crap. I'd love to see you. I'm sorry. It's been a weird day. I'm really not this much of a dork," Broc stumbled, spilling his drink in his lap. "It's okay, I understand. Life tends to do that to us from time to time," Valentina stated, handing him some napkins.

"Are you fucking kidding me? She's into me. A girl like that is into ME," Broc thought. Broc couldn't decide if it was his new look or his new attitude. Either way, this experience gave him a new perspective on life, skin color, and the color brown. He would not have noticed Valentina in the same light before his transformation.

But because he was consciously aware of his external differences, he felt more comfortable talking to people that he didn't feel comfortable talking to so candidly when he was in his former skin.
Los Angeles, California
Thursday, April 12th 10:01 a.m.

Mr. James West was under fire for some racist comments made about the most recent police brutality case. James said that the "boy probably was doing something wrong. Someone that looks like that doesn't belong where he was." The boy in question was a biracial Spanish/Mexican American. His skin was darker than other Spaniards due to his South American side.

James saw darker skin as a sign of crime, poverty, and illness. He didn't care if you were Hispanic, Chinese, or Black. Of course, he was cordial when he met Barack Obama, but deep down he still wanted to find something wrong with the former President of the United States, simply because half of him was Black. But as long as it was making James money, he did his best to keep his mouth closed. But bigots never know how to completely keep their opinions to themselves. It always seeps out through the cracks in their usually chapped, racist skin. They claim God hates ugly after all.

52

James being the bigot that he is was consistently in the news. An organization called, "SPREAD LOVE" challenged him to show up for a live webcast to talk about some of the statements that he has made about the disabled, poor, and other ethnic groups. Spread Love is an organization that does not discriminate others based on skin color, abilities, religious beliefs, economic status, sexual identity, sexual orientation, or age. Spread Love is one of the most diverse groups of it's kind around. The type of diversity that actually inhabits the people it says are allowed. All walks of life host seminars, peaceful protests, and spread love throughout the world in attempts to make an impact of change.

"Do you feel that we are all created equal," the Arabic-American representative of Spread Love asked. "I believe that some of us have more opportunities than others and we have responsibilities to be the example, to protect the rest," James West, CEO of Matador Enterprises responded.

"You didn't answer my question, Mr. West," Sasha insisted, leaning in with a head tilt. "I know I didn't. There's nothing I can say to please you people. Let me ask YOU a question. Where are you from," James asks.

"I'm from Chicago. I grew up right outside of Schaumburg, Illinois," Sasha responds. "No. What country are you from," James corrected. "I'm from America and so are my parents. I was born here," Sasha says.

"Impossible. People like you aren't born here," James ignorantly responds. "People like me? What are people like me? Does my skin color frighten you? Does Leila's skin frighten you because she's Black? Does Thomas make you feel safer because he looks more like you," Sasha says pointing at her colleagues for the panel. "History answers all of your questions. People that look like me aren't bombing public places, hi-jacking planes, and terrorizing America," James says.

"Are you kidding? Men that look like you, caucasian men are

responsible for the majority of the mass shootings in America. Local terrorism. Not Black men. Not Muslims. Or people with dark skin. It's people that look like you. This has NOTHING to do with how we all look. The problem is white male patriarchy. Many of the people that look like you have been taught that they are better. It's racism, sexism, privilege, and a shit ton of entitlement. This country was built on Black American's labor as slaves. Martin Luther King explained that no other ethnic group has been a slave on American soil. You say Black people are lazy. But when they were freed as slaves, they were given NOTHING to get started on. So yes, many of them are left behind, struggling and just trying to survive. Starting from nothing is the complete opposite of how America treated people with lighter skin like yours. The white man. And NO it's not your fault. But you are perpetuating the same cycle that got a lot of people in the situations that they are in. Silence on issues that matter is also known as compliance, MISTER WEST," Sasha concluded, catching her breath.

"Well that was an ear-full. Let me ask you something. You're Muslim, right? Why do you care so much about the plight of Black people," James asked, using hand gestures.

"First of all, no. I am not Muslim. Muslim is a religion. My ethnicity is not a religion. I am an Arabic woman who was born in America. I care not solely for the Black people of this country. I care for all people of all countries to be treated equally. No one is better than anyone. Not even you. I came here feeling like maybe there was some good in you. But now I just feel sorry for you. You don't even know who you are," Sasha said, upset.

"Turn the camera off," one of the Spread Love representatives stated. "No. Keep it rolling," Thomas responded.

"May I interject for a moment," Thomas, the caucasian representative asked. "Sure, Thomas, go ahead," James said with a calm, confident smile.

"Have you ever done some research on where you came from?

Submitted your DNA to one of those large ancestry organizations to see what countries of origin your ancestors are from. To see what's going through your bloodline," Thomas asked James. "No. I cannot say that I have. I've never cared. I can look at myself and see that it's Europe. I'm a true American. I don't need the other specifics," James said.

"A true American from Europe, huh? Okay. Looking at me, what do you think my background is? The way someone looks is not always a determinant to who they are, you know. What people are goes deeper than what's seen on the outside. Humans are complicated creatures," Thomas explained.

"I would say that you're a white man. Anyone with eyes can see that," James responded, plainly. "I am partially white. That is true. It was the box I checked for many years on job applications. But I also have roots in Indonesia and the Philippines. And I respect and value every part of me," Thomas said, returning a confident smile at James.

"I would like to conduct an experiment. Would you be willing to challenge your perspectives by participating, James," Thomas asked as the others in the room stared.

"What type of experiment," James inquired, rubbing his chin. "We all have submitted a DNA sample to A.N.D. D.N.A. where we can trace anyone's ethnic background compilations, epigenetic patterns, and biological components. We learn who we are by knowing where we have been," Thomas responded.

"I don't think that is necessary. I know who I am," James hesitated with a frown.

"You were adopted, right," Thomas stated.
"Yes, I was adopted but those are my parents. They took great care of me for as long as I could remember. They taught me how to build wealth and left a great deal of money to me. As far as I'm concerned, they are all I need to know," James insisted.

"We came here to discuss some of your comments and actions towards people of color in the community and how damaging it is for someone with your power to use their voice to spread false stereotypes and prejudices," Sasha chimed back into the conversation after cooling off.

"Okay, I'm listening. How will giving you a sample of my DNA prove anything," James asked.

"It's just an experiment. You may be from Europe only. It's possible. But what if there's more," Sasha explained.

"Fine. Do whatever you need to do if it will amuse you and your people… community," James said using hand quotations, sarcastically.

Thomas handed James a consent form to take his samples and send them off for testing. A heavy set Samoan man in a white lab coat and blue gloves came out promptly, heading towards Mr. James West. He initiated the procedure by taking a sample of James' saliva through a swab inside of his cheek. He concluded the sample with blood and hair.

"Are we done," James asked.

"Yes, we will be in touch. Thank you for taking the time to speak with us, Sasha concluded. James only cared about money and he didn't want to lose any. He didn't think his views were as problematic as they were. With the increasing success of MATADOR, he felt invincible. But appealing to the poor by showing up for certain causes couldn't hurt… right?

CHAPTER SIX: FERIA DE ABRIL DE SEVILLA

Shanghai, 7:02 p.m. Same Day. Thursday, April 12th

Parker and Rebecca were doing no better than before. Parker was becoming weaker and more lethargic than the day prior. Rebecca's face began to droop even more as if she had undergone a stroke. Her words slurred, furthering the frustration in communication between the two curse-stricken siblings.

"What do you expect me to do," Rebecca said, growing impatient with her brother's ignorance. "Just let me lay here until Broc comes back with the cure," Parker stated. In just a matter of hours Parker had made a fort in the middle of the floor. On the floor with him were pillows, blankets, food, and an absolute mess as he could not move fast enough to do much.

His room reeked of urine despite his attempts to drag himself into the bathtub facing the Oriental Pearl Tower. He did occupy the largest bedroom of the suite.

"You look and smell like shit, Parker. There's no guarantee Broc is going to have some magical cure. We may have to wait this out until old Zinga comes back to her shop," Rebecca said with her hand over her mouth.

"Oh, I look like shit? Isn't that ironic. Have you taken a gaze into a silver spoon lately? You're a plastic surgeon's nightmare, Becky. Hideous," Parker snapped back.

Defeated, Rebecca head back to her room and began to take more pills, hoping to numb it away.

Friday, April 13th
12:00 a.m. Seville, Spain (Time zone change)
6:00 a.m. in Shanghai

Checking back in with Broc who by now was thousands of miles away donning his new golden brown Earth-suit and curly, big, afro hair.

His plane finally arrived Seville, Spain on his mission to meet with Mr. Sebastian Barrio at Plaza de Torros de Sevilla.

Upon exiting the aircraft, Broc waved at Valentina who was standing by the doors to bid farewell to all of the other passengers. "See you later, Mr. West," Valentina properly addressed him.

It was about 1 am by the time Broc made it nervously through Spanish customs. He kept thinking his face would magically change again causing his passport to be invalid. As he wait for a taxi, Broc opened the front facing camera on his phone to stare into his own eyes.

The taxi driver took him to Plaza de toros de Sevilla. Broc circled the area, exploring the scene while expecting Sebastian Barrio to just appear outside the bullring and know who he was.

It was late. Broc decided to take in the Spanish traditions that were surrounding him. The pristine Moorish architecture, artistic landscapes adorned with colorful flowers, and the people. Hours passed. Broc had taken a nap in an abandoned phone booth that he found.

11:00 a.m.

Everyone was dressed in their best attire. It looked like another world. The Feria de Abril de Sevilla was taking place. This festival was customary in Seville and usually begins two weeks after Holy Week. A small city in the midst of an already established city erected and was scheduled to last for approximately one week.

The men were wearing costumes that made them all look like bullfighters; a short jacket, tight trousers, and boots. The women were all wearing colorful Flamenco dresses with their hair styled. Decorative casetas were all over the area. Horses and carriages and a pop-up amusement park with rides and games. Broc became aware that a fair was taking place. He arrived just in time for it to begin. It was a celebration of music, food, flamenco, and life. Still no sign of Mister Sebastian Barrios.

2:02 p.m.

Hours passed. Broc entered a small restaurant. "So sorry. We are closing," a young woman said as other customers were walking out. "But it's 2pm," Broc said looking at the clock on the wall.
"Sí. It's time for siesta. We will reopen at 5pm," the dark haired lady smiled plainly. Relieved that she spoke English, Broc made mental note of the restaurant upon exit in case he needed to find her again.

Broc exited the restaurant and abruptly ran into a very tall, slender gentleman with very curly short hair and curious eyes.

"Pardon, Sir," the gentleman stated apologizing for running into Broc. "No worries," Broc responds. The gentleman started walking in the opposite direction of Broc, looking back at him a few times before turning the corner.

Broc decided to turn around and follow him. "Hey. Excuse me. Do you speak English," Broc asked after catching up with the gentle, slender man. "I do, amigo. Are you lost," the gentleman asked. "Not exactly, but I'm looking for someone. Do you know where I can find a man by the name of Sebastian Barrio? I think he

59

works there," Broc said pointing at the Plaza de Toros de Sevilla.

"Of course. I can take you to him," the gentleman smiled. "Thanks," Broc said, following closely behind. The man continued to look back just as he had before, to make sure that Broc was still following him. The streets were loud and filled with laughter, music, and festivities. Everyone was enjoying life as Broc turned inward to the chaos that stirred within.
It was difficult not to notice the colorful scene. One could get drunk on its beauty.

"Right this way, Sir," the gentleman said, leading Broc through a hidden door attached to the bull ring plaza. On the other side of that door, they entered an immaculate museum area that featured paintings of the original bullfights, and statues of military men with trumpets in their hands. There was a bull statue in the middle of the room with roses at it's feet. Deeper inside the stadium there were matador costumes all over the walls and capes inside of glass cases for all to see.

"Half a million people will be attending the bullfights this week," the slender man whispered as Broc awed the atmosphere. "That's cool. Do you like..work here or something," Broc asked. "Or something," the man responded. "I mean, you knew how to get in here without standing in that line out there. So you must work here, right," Broc asked, becoming uncomfortable. "I'm only taking you where you asked to be taken, Sir," the gentleman responded as he also became lost in the art surrounding them.

"Which one is your favorite," the gentleman asked as Broc stared at the matador costumes. "I like that one. The gold design pops out kind of multi- dimensional. I'd wear that one if I were a bullfighter," Broc said. There was a golden matador suit inside of a display case. Broc got closer to observe the details that go into the delicate stitch work. Golden leaves and golden flowers stitched by hand with silver rhinestones and colorful beads of decor. Silver thread was intertwined in the golden thread in a maze of swirls, intricate designs, and lace. The rhinestones, gems, and beads made the jacket appear to glow like a suit that was made of lights.

"Look at this stitchwork. This is incredible," Broc said, fawning over the Matador suit.

"Okay, yes Yes, it is," the gentleman responded twisting his head towards another exit door. The slender man nodded his head.

"And what about you, which one would you wear," Broc asked, trying to match the small talk.

"The suits are lined with silk. The silk absorbs the blood so that the fighter may wear the suit over and over again. They are very expensive," the slender man explained, nodding his head again.

"Oh, wow. That's crazy," Broc said, fascinated. Broc placed his hands on the glass for a closer look.

"Right this way, Sir," the gentleman said, leading Broc through another secret door. The door opened and closed quickly revealing nothing but darkness and a tunnel that lead downward. Spiderwebs and darkness surrounded Broc and the slender man. Broc's heart rate began to increase but he knew he had to follow in order to reach Mr. Barrio. The gentleman lit a match. The smell of fire permeated the air down the dark tunnel. Oxygen seemed thinner down there. The gentleman held the match and reached for a torch that was perched against the wall waiting to be ignited. He lit the torch with the match as the fire quickly rose up into the ceiling.

Yellow, red, and orange heat danced on the torch like a ghost that had been awakened from a tomb that it was locked in for many centuries. Black smoke burned their eyes until the flame calmed down. The slender man guided their way down the dark underground tunnel, occasionally pushing spider webs to the side. The ground was wet in places. Splashes of water, made their way to Broc's ankles with every other step that he took.

Broc let out a large scream. A large gray rat ran passed his feet. Moments later the rest of the rat family appeared to follow behind, disappearing beneath the fire lit tunnel.

"Watch your step," the gentleman whispered. After several moments, Broc and the elusive man approached another door with an electronic scanner. The man placed his eyes near the retinal scanner so that his eyes could be scanned for entry. Iris recognition is a biometric identification system uses mathematical-pattern recognition on videos of each of the eyes. Everyone's eyes are composed of complex patterns that are unique and can often be seen from a distance.

The door opened after his identity was confirmed. On the other side of the door was a futuristic white room that looked like a cross between an art gallery and a science lab. Half of the room was painted white and the other half of the room was painted blood red. This room was adorned with photos of bullfights and artwork like the museum in the main plaza hall. There were approximately 20 paintings side by side on 2 of the 4 walls. The other 2 walls remained bare. Several paintings were paired with photos. In those photos was the slender man as the bull fighter.

Becoming more nervous at the drastic change in scenery, Broc leaning in to the pictures, asks, "Is that you? What's going on? Where is Sebastian Barrio?"

"I did as I promised and brought you to him. This is who I used to be. Matador Sebastian Barrio at your service, Sir," Sebastian stated using a red cape as he took a theatrical bow.

"You knew it was me the whole time and played this game," Broc asked, with his voice cracking.

"Yes. I like to have some fun every now and then. I have been following you since your taxi arrived town. Not many people look like you here so when I got the word that an African was wandering near the plaza, I knew it was you. You were easy to find," Sebastian stated with a laugh. He had one dimple. His amusement brought it out of his face.

"Because I'm BLACK I was easy to find? That sounds racist," Broc retorts. "Oh. Does it," Sebastian snides. "I get it already, okay," Broc says, crossing his arms defensively.

"Let's get on with this, shall we," Sebastian says as he glides across the room gracefully, almost as if he were dancing.

Broc eyed the paintings from the other side of the room. They were placed on the two red walls in what appeared to be a planned pattern.

"Do you know the relationship between the matador and the bull? I was a famous bullfighter for several years before I truly learned what the relationship was. I only knew what was told to me," Sebastian began, looking off in the distance with pride.

"So you're about to tell me something that will only be what is told to me as well, I take it," Broc responded, agitated.

"Slightly. I'm going to SHOW you what the relationship is," Sebastian stated as his hands slid across a painting of a matador with a dead bull in his embrace.

"Listen, my sister, my brother and I are in danger. We are under a spell and need to turn back. I was sent here to reverse it. To save us. I'm sick of the fucking games. Can you help us or not," Broc stammered, heading towards the door.

"Mmm. That door doesn't open without my consent, Sir. And you don't leave until your mission is completed. So I suggest you relax and stay a while. You want the spell reversed, then you will follow my instructions very carefully, understood," Sebastian said, reaching for a handshake from Broc.

"I'm not shaking your fucking hand, bro. You're conning me. Let me out of here," Broc exclaimed getting louder and louder.

"No one can hear you, Sir. These walls, they are sound proof. Here, I'll put on some music," Sebastian stated as he waved his hand passed a silver speaker. The sounds of trumpets and traditional guitars permeated the air. Bullfighting music. Sebastian began to dramatically dance around the futuristic room glancing into his own eyes in the paintings from time to time. Sebastian's moves looked like he was miming the bull fight while also dancing the salsa or meringue. Occasionally finding himself right in the mathematical center of the red and the white room, Sebastian looked just like a painting.

"HELP. CAN ANYONE HEAR ME," Broc yelled banging on the bare white walls.

"Hmm. No. No one can hear you, Sir. Do you not like Bullfighting music? How about some Mozart then. Will that shut you up," Sebastian said in a thick accent while changing stations on the music player.

Broc finally tired of hearing himself yell and sat down on a brown leather couch near the door. Sighing in frustration and annoyed at watching Sebastian dance now to classical music, Broc asked, "What do you need me to do?"

"First I need your full cooperation, Sir. I need you to listen very carefully or this will not work. Do you know the relationship with the matador and the bull," Sebastian asked again, looking very adamant to be answered.

"All I know is that the bull fighter guy dances around, antagonizing the bull with a red cloth or something. The bull charges at him and the matador dude tries not to die," Broc states, growing impatient.

"Close. The bullfighting tradition has been in Spain since ancient days. It can be traced back to year 711. Bullfighting began with the Moors in Andalucia. This tradition began as bull worship and sacrifice. It's a hunting game. Man has done this for centuries. Man has done this to man. Killing for sport. Killing out of fear...."

"But what gives man the right to kill another living, breathing being? Are there no other ways to be entertained? Is he who kills exalted above those that he kills? See, the thing is… the bull just wants to play. He just wants to escape. Is it fair that he is killed upon looking for an exit, ….Broc," Sebastian continues.

"But you were a bullfighter, weren't you? And now you have strong convictions on bullfighting? That seems rather hypocritical, SIR. You bring me in here to see all of your narcissistic paintings and awards only to tell me that bullfighting isn't fair," Broc says, taking an interest in a bull plush toy that accompanies him on the leather couch.

"Yes. That's what I did. All of it is true. Every part of our history leads us to discover who we really are. The things that we are taught are not always what are right. I now keep these paintings as a tribute to the lives that were taken. The lives that I took. I respect them. I am not celebrating their death. I am celebrating their lives now. It is possible for people to change, even those accused of horrible deeds. We are human after all," Sebastian concluded as he pranced around the room in his very, very tightly fitted festival attire.

"I understand. I get it. Can I go now? Is there a magic potion I can drink or something to do to reverse this. I don't want to be Black or Brown anymore," Broc said with his head down. "Why not, the girls they like a little tan, no," Sebastian asks, giving Broc a playful nudge to the shoulder as if they were participating in locker room talk.

"Isn't it obvious? The same reason you said that you saw me the moment my taxi arrived. Wherever you go, all eyes are on you and not always for the right reasons. I don't like that kind of attention. It feels weird," Broc said.

"How do you think that started? It has to come from

somewhere, right? People started treating people that looked differently one way and others jumped in. It became their version of normal. Humans are sheep, Sir. They see one doing and they follow suit. Most humans are afraid of things that they don't understand. Thus, fear makes the 'Wolf appear bigger'. I saw that in a book somewhere," Sebastian said, reasoning with Broc as Mozart played on in the speakers in each corner of the room.

"You're right, I guess. I never thought of it that way before. I never had to," Broc said, standing up, with the bull toy still in his hands.

"You are here by no accident. You are here to be my subject. My student. I will have you here until you pass the test. Once you pass the test you can go back to Shanghai to be with your sister and brother," Sebastian began, beginning to sound like a yoga instructor.

Sebastian then pushed an obscure button which revealed a complex work station complete with an interesting looking circular chair, various computer screens, and an abundance of lab equipment.

"Are you like a scientist now that the Matador thing didn't work out," Broc asked, observing all of the peculiar devices on the white painted side of the room.

"Please sit. Trust me. That's the only way this will work," Sebastian said, directing Broc to sit in the odd shaped chair.

Broc sat carefully into the chair as metal straps locked his arms in. "This is only for your safety, Sir," Sebastian explained, tightening the straps.

Sebastian put alcohol on a cotton swab and wiped off the back of Broc's neck, and each of his arms. He placed an i.v. into one of his arms and another mysterious blue liquid into the other i.v.

"This may sting a little bit," Sebastian stated as he placed a small, silver mushroom shaped device onto the back of Broc's neck. It was about an inch big. Big enough to be placed into his brain stem at the top of his spinal cord. "What's that," Broc asked. "It's a mini computer that can create an augmented reality where you can function and move about the same way that you do here. You'll be able to taste, touch, smell, see… and even fuck if you so desire. Everything you have here you can have there. It attaches to your nervous system and better than a lucid dream, it places you there," Sebastian said, fidgeting with a long metal stick that looked like a mini sword.

"So this is like a video game? You're making me play in a virtual reality," Broc asked, relaxing into the chair.

"No, no. This is not a virtual reality. This is another reality. This sir, is real. You are going into MATADOR BULL RING, 5.0," Sebastian assured him with a sinister laugh.

"Okay. So what now," Broc asked.

"Now, I am going to cover your eyes and tap you into the bullring. Your first objective is to fight the bull. If you successfully complete your mission, I will keep my promise. You can go home. If you do not successfully fight the bull, you will die. Whatever happens in the game, happens in real life. Death and life. They are the same. You close your eyes in one world and wake up in another. Whatever you feel, your body won't know the difference in realities. It will become real for you," Sebastian explained.

"I don't know how to fight a bull," Broc said, worried.

"We all fight bull every once in a while, no? Do you know how to salsa, Sir," Sebastian asked, swinging his hips as he was earlier.

"A little bit, I guess," Broc said as the lost child look emerged once more on his face.

"Then you can fight a bull. Just dance. Place the sword between his shoulders. Through his heart when you're done though. It may take a while," Sebastian concluded, trying not to laugh.

"And if the bull wins," Broc asks.

"Then you die," Sebastian says simply.

"Now listen. Just breathe. I'm going to walk you through the beginning. After that you're on your own," Sebastian continues as he places a red blindfold over Broc's eyes. Sebastian then presses a button on the back of the apparatus on the back of Broc's now sweating neck. Beads of sweat and body hair surrounded the apparatus as it dialed in. A golden spark flew from the back of the mushroom as Sebastian pressed the button again.

"Oh my god. It's so real," Broc says, opening his eyes into the alternate reality inside of a gorgeous bullring.

"What do you see," Sebastian asks.

"I see lots of people screaming in joy. I see dirt in the air. Dirt at my feet. Fluffy clouds. Blue skies. I'm wearing the costume I pointed at earlier! The one from the museum. It's even more beautiful than it was in the glass case. Where's the bull," Broc asks, nervously.

The matador costume glowed the way minced golden powder would underneath the Spanish sun.

"Oh. Don't worry. He's coming. You have three tercios (stages) or rounds. Each will be announced by the sound of a trumpet. Now, remember what I told you. Fight the bull," Sebastian finishes as he presses one final button on a remote device, temporarily blocking communication with he and Broc to complete his mission.

CHAPTER SEVEN: LA CORRIDA

Broc is in the alternate augmented reality bull ring wearing a fancy multi-dimensional gold matador costume; the traje de luces (The suit of lights). Each intricate detail more noticeable than before. Still fascinated by his altered senses, he looks around taking in the other world. He inhales and exhales. The dust enters his lungs. He can feel it. He can taste the dry dirt. The sandy dirty feels gritty between his teeth as it lingers in the air.

Broc hears someone yell, "Matador Negro! A Black Matador!" The colorful crowd roars with excitement. They were cheering for him to win. Still nervous, he kicks the dirt around.

Broc begins the parade by saluting the dignitary presiding over the bullfight. A moment passes and suddenly he hears the signal that the first round of the bullfight will begin. A trumpet is heard in very close range. His ears begin ringing, unbearably. "Sebastian? It's so loud. Can you turn it down…," Broc began, hoping that Sebastian could still hear him.

The bull enters the ring following the trumpet sound. He looks larger than Broc imagined. His furry coat looked like it had just been polished. Each of the hairs had a life of their own on his big black bull body. Broc is able to observe how strong and fierce the bull is as the other participants antagonize the bull in attempts to tire him out.

The trumpet sounds a second time which marks the beginning of the second stage. In this stage, three banderilleros attempt to take two sharp sticks (banderillas) and stick them into the bull's shoulders to make him weaker and also more angry. If the bull cannot lift his head, his horns are not as deadly.

Each banderillero displays his dominance over the bull by beginning with a dance just before charging towards the bull.

Broc watching everything taking place knows that the third and final round must be his if he wishes to reverse the curse.

The trumpet sounds a third time marking the beginning of the third and final round. Tercio de muerte. Broc's heart pounded like a stampede of a thousand bulls was taking place inside of his body. Inhale.

"Are you ready to dance, Gweilo," a voice whispers from a place that he cannot see. Broc still tasting the gritty dirt in his mouth, looks around for Zinga, the last person to refer to him as that name. He sees nothing but a crowd full of 40,000 people waiting to witness what some would call an art, others would call a cruel sacrifice in the name of entertainment.

The crowds cheering became more audible. He could hear their words as if they were standing directly beside him. Some cheered in excitement, while others made racist comments. "Fight the bull, monkey," one man yelled.

"The nigger is going to die in the fight."
"Two animals fight to the death."

"Go back to Africa, ugly monkey!"

"I'm AMERICAN," Broc screamed out in rage, feeling defeated before the battle, in his current Earth-suit.

"NO ONE CARES. KILL THE BULL," another screamed.

"NO! KILL THE NIGGER," another laughed.

Broc enters the ring, this time with a silver sword and a red satin cape hanging over a wooden rod. The bull stood about 15 feet away. Broc fans his muleta to taunt the bull as he had seen done in television. The bull playfully charges forward towards the blood red cape.

Broc successfully dances around the bull, avoiding being hit. He becomes arrogantly pleased with his instinct and begins a celebratory dance, mimicking the moves displayed by Sebastian earlier.

Broc trips and falls as the crowd roars in an undetermined excitement. It was hard to tell anymore who they were cheering for. As Broc stumbles to his feet and stood up, his eyes met with the bull. Dirt now surrounded them both like a cloud on a humid day. The bull's eyes had a human softness in them. A softness that begged for the same mercy it took upon Broc's vulnerable moment on the ground when the bull could have killed him. The bull's eyes appear to say, "I know what we're here for. Please don't kill me."

Broc tries to remind himself that this is just a game. Inner monologue resumes. "It's not real. Anything I kill here does not really die."

Sebastian's voice echoes from earlier, "Whatever happens in the game, happens in real life. Death and life are the same. You close your eyes in one world and wake up in another."

The sword begins to visibly tremble in Broc's embrace. The sweat from his upper lip began to seep between them. Salty, gritty lips. Broc licks his lips to moisturize their dryness.

"SEBASTIAN! Let me out, bro! I cannot do this. He doesn't deserve to die," Broc screamed out, again hoping that Mr. Sebastian Barrio would hear his call.

The silence in waiting became louder than the roars of thousands. Sebastian did not respond. Looking into the bull's eyes became unavoidable as Broc stood there attempting to communicate telepathically with a computer generated beast he had now determined was sentient.

Stiff, he stood for what felt like days; he and the bull staring into one another's souls, contemplative.

Everything suddenly went black.

"Sir, what happened," Sebastian asked, removing the red cloth from Broc's eyes as he sat still strapped into the chair. It took Broc a moment to adjust his eyes to the light and adjust his mind to the other reality.

"It's me Sebastian. You're back in my office again. Why didn't you kill the bull," Sebastian asked. "I couldn't do it," Broc whispered clearing his throat as the words barely came out. He hadn't used his voice in days. Sebastian unfastened the straps and handed Broc a bottle of water. Broc swallowed the water in one gulp.

"How long have I been in here," Broc asked. "Four days," Sebastian responded, now filing his nails with a feminine designed nail file. "But it felt like hours," Broc said, bewildered as he reached for a second bottle of water.

"I know," Sebastian said.

"I can't kill him because he doesn't want to die. He doesn't deserve to die. He's a living being. Why should he die," Broc whispers, choking on his words.

"Because that's how it's always been. It's tradition. It's custom," Sebastian says.

"Do you really feel that way? Can't customs be changed? I won't do it," Broc says, finishing his third bottle of water and observing the I.V. still planted into his arm.

"No. I don't believe that way anymore. I told you. I no longer fight. I no longer kill. This is part of my mission. To teach what it is to respect life. All lives. Those we see, those we meet, and those that we eat," Sebastian says.

"Eat," Broc asked.

"They eat the bull after the battle, Broc. I know you're hungry by now. Will you be dining with us," Sebastian asks.

"Yes. No. Of course I'm hungry. But I'm not eating or killing that bull," Broc exclaims, attempting to get up from the chair. Sebastian slams him back into the chair and carefully whispers, "you will complete your mission so that I can complete mine."

CHAPTER EIGHT: PASSPORT

Broc takes a deep breath as Sebastian fastens his arms back into the seat and covers his eyes again. When he opens his eyes, he is back in the bull ring again. This time he sees a Matador in a sky blue and gold suit standing ahead of him who is much taller than him. He feels a stinging pain in his shoulders. As he makes eye contact with the matador, the matador looks away, disinterested in emotionally connecting. He listens again as the crowd roars. Their screams are the bass felt through the ground causing the alternate reality to move.

Just as Broc looks to his feet and sees his hooves instead of boots, he hears Sebastian's voice, "Now, Sir. you will BE the bull."

Broc begins to shake nervously while fitting into his new body. His legs where arms used to be. He could feel the incredible strength built in this new body but it terrified him, like a transgendered man with the first dose of artificial testosterone. He wanted to fuck. He wanted to fight. Anything and everything in sight. Broc the Bull ran in circles around the bull ring. There was nowhere to hide for a beast that large. There were no decorative walls to slide and hide behind like those for the humans in the bull ring.

The same privileges did not exist for the hunted.

He was open and exposed for all to see and to harm if they so choose.

The Matador danced with his sword and muleta in the middle of the ring in efforts to seduce Broc the bull to charge towards him.

Los Angeles, California, United States of America
Tuesday, April 17th 7:15 a.m.

Lucy and James West were at home in Beverly Hills enjoying a sunlit breakfast. "A refill, Mr. West," the butler asked refilling James' 'MAKE AMERICA GREAT AGAIN' coffee mug. "Yes, please," James responded, pushing his cup forward.

"Honey, there's a phone call for you," Lucy said handing the landline phone to her husband.
"This is James."

"Hello James. This is Thomas from Spread Love Inc. Is now a good time to speak," Thomas asked.

"As good of time as any," James responded, sipping his hot drink.

"Great. We would be honored if you were able to come in and speak with us again. We have some exciting things that we would like you to be a part of. Matador could be a great asset to Spread Love," Thomas said with a smile, appealing to James' interests.

"Oh?"

"Yes. We would like to learn more about your company and perhaps we could educate each other. We'd also like to give you your confidential DNA results," Thomas explained.

"Well, you know what. That sounds great. If Matador Enterprises can help anyone, I'm all about it. Especially an organization such as yours," James said, rolling his eyes but maintaining a sincere tone.

"Friday, April 27th, 10am good for you," Thomas asked.

"Sure. I'll be there," James responded, hanging up the phone.

Shanghai, China
Tuesday, April 17th 9:01 a.m.

Things continued along the brachistochrone curve, also known as the shortest time of fastest descent. Rebecca's words were barely understood as her body rapidly continued to deform and crumple into itself. Parker had now parked himself in one spot and given up on dragging himself through the suite for any reason. As you can imagine, the stench was rotten.

"Look at this! Only one of the cases of altered human state resulted in a reversal. A swimmer about 10 years ago. Says he was turned into a dolphin before winning the olympics," Parker read aloud.

"That sounds stupid. Why would Zinga turn anyone into a dolphin," Rebecca responded wiping drool from her mouth.

"Maybe this case was a favorable one. Maybe it wasn't Zinga," Parker said.

"Have you heard from Broc yet? It's been days. I've texted him a few times and nothing," Rebecca asked looking concerned, and opening the curtains.

"No. I'm sure he's fine. Either way, there's not much we can do here. Wait... Another case here... Nebraska. A farmer from the 1960's was turned into a black man. He died of a heart attack moments after it was reversed, according to this account told by one of his children. Henry Jackson was his name. I wonder if we can find him," Parker rambled on, getting excited again.

Friday, April 20th 3:33 p.m.
Seville, Spain

Broc the bull stands looking strong on the outside, yet trembling with fear on the inside. His black bull fur coat glistened underneath the Spanish sunlight.

"I will die in this video game," his inner monologue asserts. He continued to run circles in the bullring as the crowd roared impatiently. The matador unfazed, still danced to a song that only he could hear. It must have been techno because he didn't move as gracefully as Sebastian.

"I HAVE TO KILL HIM FOR MY BROTHER AND MY SISTER," Broc decided, charging towards the Matador. Swiftly the Matador moved away while lunging his sword towards the aggressive bull. Broc the bull had been hit. He groaned but did not fall to the ground.

"You will be my dinner tonight," the matador whispered, licking his lips seductively. Broc charged at him again, aiming for the matador instead of the red cape.

With his shoulders stinging from the incision, Broc charged forward again. This time when he charged, he hit the matador, flipping him into the air and onto his back. Brown dust flew into the air, slowly disappearing.

"That's enough," Broc the bull thought hoping he would be heard.

Sebastian heard Broc's cry and paused the game once more, taking him back into his usual reality.

"Good Evening, Sir. You have completed the mission. You

have been on both sides as the Matador and as the bull. The spell will wear off soon," Sebastian stated, removing the metal straps from Broc's arms.

Broc took several glances at the red and white room before the two exited and began their upwards trek from underneath the bullring.

Through the dark tunnels again, they walked, stepping over dead rats and shooing away spiders. Eyes lit up in the distant darkness that Broc hoped were also just rodents...

Silence surrounded them as they both exited the secret tunnel underneath the Plaza de Torres de Sevilla.

"That's it. I can go now," Broc asked surprised, rubbing his shoulder where he had been hit as the bull.

"Yes. That's it for now. Zinga will find you when it's time," Sebastian replied, escorting Broc through the tunnel, and out the secret door to the busy street once more.

9:15 p.m.

It was the final night of the festival. The colorful town was still filled with people wearing their colorful clothing and wide smiles. Fireworks began above. It was Broc's first time realizing how much fireworks looked like flowers in bloom. Beginning as a bud and then opening as wide as it could before disappearing into the night. Broc chuckled in awe at how beautiful everything was now. His eyes were opened. REALLY OPENED.

"Broc! BROC! I found you," a voice in the distance shouted.

Echoing words of a familiar voice emerged from the festival tents. It was the most beautiful woman Broc had ever seen.

"Valentina, how did you..." Broc began. "You're hard to lose with all of that hair...," Valentina smiled.

"You like it," Broc asked, still not used to his textured mane.

"I love it," Valentina replied reaching for Broc's hand.

The two held hands as metallic fireworks bloomed overhead. Some of the fireworks morphed into familiar shapes like hearts, rings, and the kamuro, a popular Japanese hairstyle that appeared to pour out of the sky like fire from outer space.

"So what have you been doing this entire time," Valentina asked.

"Sightseeing," Broc responded, sounding almost like a question.

"Did you see anything worth remembering," Valentina asked.

"Yes. I saw a lot. I learned a lot. A LOT," Broc began, squeezing Valentina's hand.

"What are YOU doing in Seville," Broc continued, curiously.

"There's a festival going on. I come every year when I can. I love the energy in the town. The fireworks… I was hoping I would find you. You weren't answering your texts the past couple of days…," Valentina asserted as the two walked down the busy streets.

"Oh. Yeah. Sorry. I was a little preoccupied," Broc explained, checking his phone.

Broc saw several missed text messages and phone calls from Shanghai. He couldn't let the chance of having an affair with the gorgeous flight attendant distract him from his duties.

"Will you excuse me a moment," Broc asked.

"No worries," Valentina said with a polite nod.

Shanghai, China (6 hours ahead)
Saturday, April 21st 3:47 a.m.

Laying in a pool of urine, Parker sat still doing research on his condition and as usual staying up to date on world issues.

The phone rang.

"BROC! It's been like a week dude. What's the deal? What's going on? Are you okay? Is Zinga with you? Are you still Black," Parker exclaimed, despite the fact that it was just after 3am in Shanghai.

"Dude, relax. Gimme a second," Broc began, watching Valentina talk with the locals from a distance.

"RELAX?! Fucking relax? I'm God-damned paralyzed from the waist down. Your sister looks like the fucking elephant man… and you're ignoring our calls and messages as if it's no big deal. Are you fucking insane? Or just some dumb ass nigger now," Parker said.

Broc's entire body began to shake with rage as he glanced at Valentina who stood with a warm smile on her face a few feet away.

Instead of causing a scene, Broc instantly shut his phone off and put it back in his pocket.

"RE-BEC-CA! Come in here," Parker yelled, throwing his belongings around.

Entering the room with a bottle of vodka, Rebecca stared at Parker for a few moments. "What do you want, brother," Rebecca responded, sarcastically.

"Broc shut his phone off again. We were talking and he hung

up on me. I need you to go find that kid. The Asian kid that gave him the new passport," Parker demanded.

"Well. I overheard you calling him names. Your shitty attitude is going to keep you stuck this way," Rebecca snapped, still slurring her words through her disfigured face.

"Sorry. I'm just.. frustrated," Parker began as angry tears started falling from his face.

"What about the Henry Jackson guy? Are you going to find him to investigate what happened to his father? I don't think we're going to find that little Asian kid again. What did Broc say? Is he coming back with a cure," Rebecca continued.

"No. I don't know. He sounds busy. I'm not even sure what he's doing now," Parker responded, still fuming.

"Just give him some time and stop being a dick. He'll call back," Rebecca assured him.

"Okay. Now what," Parker asked.

Rebecca head towards the double doors and said, "I have an appointment. I'll be back."

Though it was late, Rebecca donned her jeweled face mask and hit the Shanghai streets, reading the information on a business card in her mangled hands.

The card read, 'Dr. Lee'.

FLASH. FLASH. FLASH.

CHAPTER NINE: NEW EYES

Madrid, Spain
Thursday, April 26th 1:15 p.m.

Several days passed. Valentina and Broc had been spending time getting to know one another. Every day Broc awakened, he worried that he would be someone else, someone that Valentina would not recognize. A friend of Valentina's was away for a few weeks and let Valentina stay at their home in Madrid. Valentina was on holiday and invited Broc to join.

They spent their days exploring the city, picnicking in luscious green parks, visiting museums and famous landmarks. They were falling in love with each other quickly. Broc felt ashamed that he was hiding a secret from her. Broc didn't know how Valentina would feel about him in his former Earth-Suit, so he decided to enjoy the time with her while he could. Or at least until the spell wore off, as it was promised to happen soon.

"What do you think about moving to Barcelona or staying in Europe with me somewhere," Valentina asked, fluttering her lashes over her wide brown eyes.

"I would consider it. But my home is in LA. My entire family is there. What do you think about moving to the states," Broc asked. Valentina's shoulders began to droop as she responded with a, "perhaps."

"I don't want to move too fast, you know. You're an amazing woman. I've never met someone like you before. I'm willing to do whatever it takes to keep you in my life. Anything," Broc says, pulling Valentina's frown up with his hand.

"Anything? Didn't you say you wanted to live in the moment now? That this moment is all that matters? That you had some sort of revelation recently and could be your best self with me. Well I'm here now and this is now. What's stopping you," Valentina went on.

"I'm not... I'm not who you think I am, V. I ...," Broc began.

"Really? Stop being silly. I think you're perfect. You don't need to be anyone else," Valentina assured him.

"But that's just it. I'm not this. None of this is me," Broc said.

Valentina laughed and grabbed Broc by the arm and whispered, "well then who are you, Broc?"

Broc took a step away from Valentina and whispered, "I'm white."

There was silence for a long moment. For Broc this moment felt like an eternity. The silence was interrupted with a loud laugh. Valentina began laughing so hard that tears were falling from her eyes. She fell to the ground laughing and out of breath.

Rubbing his brown skin, Valentina still laughing, says, "So... does this just wash off?"

"No... Valentina. I'm white. I was white 3 weeks ago. I was born white. I'm an American white boy from Los Angeles. My father is James West, owner of Matador Enterprises. A spell was placed on me and my family. I was turned into this," Broc explained.

Another long pause ensued. Valentina began laughing again.

"I don't know if you're joking or if you're ashamed of being Black. If you are, that's really sad. I've been called white before.

White washed. Oreo. Girl who wants to be white because I speak different languages but have brown skin. It's okay, Broc. Just be you. It's you that I'm falling for, okay. I don't care if you're black, blue, or silver, " Valentina explained.

"What about white? You didn't mention white," Broc asked with a concerned eyebrow.

"Silly! Of course. I don't care if you were white either. But you're not so it doesn't matter. You're you and that's enough for me," Valentina said as her lips reached for Broc's lips and assured him with a kiss.

"You're right," Broc whispered with his eyes still closed from the kiss.

"Wait. I'm curious about something. What kind of stories have you been allowed into your psyche about Black lives and Black existence? To talk proper or eloquently does not equate with whiteness. Poverty should not be automatically associated with Black existence. There are multi-facets to all societies, all cultures. The propaganda filled media has chosen to paint those with darker skin as the lowest of the low. Especially the media that comes from your country. Have you not learned anything from these museums? Black Kings. Black Intellect. Black Inventions. Black Art. Black Riches. Royalty that looks just like YOU. Just like me. They still exist you know," Valentina reminded Broc.

"Yes. I see. I think my family... was ignorant. They weren't told the truth about a lot of things and passed the false truths on to us as children. I'm sorry if I said anything to offend you," Broc finished.

"You didn't offend me. Americans. Black Americans like yourself seem to have been brainwashed into thinking they are less than, which is not true. It's a disgusting result of white supremacy, slavery, and oppression for hundreds of years. I've always found it comical that they say America is the land of the free, when most of the minds there are enslaved. The foods are poison. The media poison," Valentina finished.

The two began walking towards the Ciculo de Belles Artes for lunch. As they walked down the street, the white buildings on either side felt like a healing energy was being released through them. An angelic statue with open arms stood atop a building that read the words, 'Metropolis'.

Broc stared at everything, taking in the views of the ancient city, the signature smell of foods, public transportation, and the bergamot citrus aroma that surrounded his polyglot tour guide.

"I like that you keep your hair natural, Valentina," Broc said still taking in the views.

"Thank you for liking it. It's natural to be natural. I figure if everyone else's natural is widely accepted, mine should be too," Valentina said, with a playful laugh.
"My hair though… it's so big. It's kind of a nuisance at times. Everyone wants to touch it. I'd cut it off but… it'll probably just grow right back," Broc said with his words trailing off remembering that the curse was still present.

"I get it. Being different can be overwhelming when you stick out," Valentina replied.

"But you're beautiful. Doesn't that help some," Broc asked, playing with the textured food that sat at the table in front of him.

"Beautiful doesn't matter. The first thing someone sees when they look at me is that I'm BLACK. The second thing they see is that I'm a woman. Beauty… comes later. And should someone who may not be traditionally beautiful be less deserving of kindness than someone who is? I've been called the ugliest names in my life. It's all about whose eyes see me. Right now, it's you," Valentina finished, taking a bit of her food. Valentina slowly ate strawberries that must have been delicious due to her smacking.

"If I didn't know any better, I'd think you hadn't been Black very long, Mr. Broc," Valentina laughed.

"Ha. Ha," Broc joined in, sarcastically.

The two sat atop the rooftop of the Circulo de Bellas Artes where they could view the entire city of Madrid.

The racism in Madrid was unbearable for Broc. The locals either acted like they did not see them or stared at them as if they were unwelcome intruders. Older people began whispering their insults loudly in their native Spanish tongue. Among the insults were things like, "You are not welcome. You should leave."

"I thought it was bad in Shanghai. How do you deal with this all the time," Broc asked Valentina who was sipping a cup of chamomile tea. "I mean, there's racism all over the world. Being a flight attendant, I sort of have built up this wall. I enjoy learning about new cultures and seeing the world. There's always going to be someone that doesn't have love for all in their hearts. I just choose to be careful wherever I go and continue the love in mine," Valentina whispered between sips of her fizzy water.

3:33 p.m.

Broc excused himself to the restroom. As he walked through the halls of the artistically designed cafe, the white lights flickered. They mimicked the colors of the Oriental Pearl Tower. Purple, orange, and blue fluorescent lights took over the long hallway that lead to the loo. A shadowy figure appeared at the end of Broc's view.

Broc swung his body around to see the world around him. Time stood still.

Either everyone had disappeared or he had stepped into another dimension higher than the third that most of us know best.

The strong scent of mandarin permeated the air, stinging the hairs inside of Broc's nose. A familiar smell had found its way.

"Broc, it is me. Zingaro. You have completed your mission. No longer a Gweilo. Ha! Are you ready to be YOU again," Zinga stated with her signature toothless grin.

"No. I don't want to be that person again. I…"

"You met someone. I know. But you have learned your lessons. The gift I gave you was new eyes. New eyes on the inside. Those eyes will stay with you," Zinga said, reaching for Broc's hand.

"But I don't want to be any of it. I won't be that person again. I want to be this one," Broc protested, pushing her hand away, softly.

"Ah? You want to stay golden, eh? You like the girl, yeah? Is that the only reason you want to be brown," Zinga asked, tilting her head to look into Broc's soul.

"Of course not. But I need more time. I need to make sure she loves me for me and I think there's things I can accomplish this way," Broc responded, assured of himself.

"Contrarily there are things you can accomplish in your OTHER Earth-suit now that you have the eyes that you have. A white man as an ally for Black lives and other minorities can create a ripple in the world. A ripple that the world needs. But I'll give you a few more days…. as you wish," Zinga said, as the lights flickered again.

"What about Rebecca and Parker? I thought my deeds would reverse their curse as well," Broc asked, with a frown of the brow.

"Ah. No. No curse. This is a gift. And for the gift to be effective, one has to complete their own journey. They…they are not done yet, Their story is not over," Zinga said in a new unfamiliar accent, adjusting her colorful head scarf.

The lights flickered once more. As Zinga vanished, the Spanish music began playing again, and the patrons reappeared. Broc stood there in thought, accidentally bumping into someone as they made their way through the long hall.

"Pardon, Sir," the guest yelled with an unwelcoming frown.

Shanghai, China (6 hours ahead of Spain)
Tuesday, May 1st 11:11 a.m.

Rebecca stood in the mirror as the bandages came off of her face. Nervously, she reached her hands to her breasts. They were plump once more. Her nipples became erect in excitement. Many days had passed. Dr. Lee had successfully brought her back to 'life'. She couldn't wait to get back to the suite at The Grand Kempinski Hotel to give the news to Parker.

"Parker! Parker! I am free! Fuck that gypsy bitch. Look at me," Becky yelled, startling her brother as she came in the door like a wrecking ball.

Parker looked his sister up and down and said simply, "You still don't have any hair."

"It'll grow back. Why can't you just be happy for me? GOD! I mean… if you could do something other than sit on the computer all day, maybe you'd see that there's a doctor that can fix your legs too," Becky retorted.

Calmly, Parker adjusted his limp body to sit upright and said, "You. Cannot. Reverse. This. Shit. Yours… mine. We need to find

Zinga."

"I reversed it just fine, actually. Sure there's still a few little things that need to be fixed. But at least I don't look like a monster anymore," Becky stated.

"Okay. If these slave owners couldn't reverse their curse from being turned into female slaves. If these nazis ... and other people couldn't reverse their curse... I just don't see the Gods having any mercy on you," Parker said, still staring into his laptop screen. His eyes were stark red from being glued to the screen for days. It felt like he had been staring directly into the sun.

Rebecca stormed off to the restroom attached to her room, slamming every door she encountered. Though housekeeping had done their best to clean the suite since their dilemma, a slight stench remained.

Staring into her own eyes in the mirror, Rebecca stood analyzing herself. She thought about what still needed to be worked on, physically- She inhaled, cupped both of her breasts in both of her hands, threw her head back, and exhaled.

The bathroom lights flickered. They were now purple, orange, and blue. In the reflection standing next to her she saw Zinga. Startled, Rebecca jumped and looked beside her. Zinga was not there. She was only in the mirror reflection standing right beside her. Rebecca opened her mouth and prepared to scream.

"Parker can't hear us. You're in my world now," Zinga whispered, staring at Rebecca from the other side of the wide bathroom mirror. Zinga moved with Rebecca as Rebecca attempted to walk away. The door slammed shut on its own.

Struggling to open the door, Rebecca pulled aggressively until her wig flew off landing at her feet. The small statured woman waited in the reflection for Rebecca to stop.

"Are you done," Zinga asked, reaching her hand through the

mirror.

"Yes. Are YOU done? Is this stupid curse done? And where the hell is my baby brother," Becky whined.

"First, I see you've made some changes. Did you think it would be that easy? Second, I'm not done until you are. Third, Broc is fine," Zinga responded.

"Then fix me, GOD DAMMIT! FIX ME NOW," Rebecca shrieked, rattling the glasses on the counter.

Zinga slid only her face through the mirror between them and whispered, "No."

With a laugh, she disappeared. Rebecca still staring into the mirror, searched all around for Zinga. The lights flickered once more. She was gone.

Rebecca went to the sink and began to splash water on her face. The refreshing wetness awakened her from what felt like a dream. As the water dried, her face morphed back into the deformed face Zinga gifted her with.

She frantically reached for her new breasts that now felt like silly putty that had been left out in the desert sun for too long.

Rebecca faced the mirror, pulled her nails down her face, and screamed, "FUCKKKK!!!"

Los Angeles, California, United States of America
10:10 am
Friday, April 27th

James West of Matador Enterprises sat in the middle of a horseshoe formation of chairs. He was joined by Sasha, Thomas, and Leila of Spread Love Inc. Cameras surrounded the room from all angles. Bright white lights shined down on the room, illuminating any and every possibility of a shadow. The lights were hot and demanded to be felt.

"Is all this lighting necessary," James asked, adjusting his tie. "Sorry about that. The lights are for the camera team to make sure we look our best. We'll turn the air up and get you some cold water to drink," Leila assured him, waving for assistance.

"We go live in 5, 4, 3, 2..."

"Welcome to this week's episode of Spread Love. Joining us today we have Mr. James West of Matador Enterprises. Hello James. How are you today," Sasha asked, cheerfully facing the cameras.

"Doing wonderful. Thank you," James replied.

"Mr. West has offered to donate some of Matador's services to Spread Love so that we may reach more viewers and continue to blast our message of love, equality, and humanity across the globe. We would like to thank him for the opportunity and meeting with us again today," Leila began.

An overwhelming applause began to flood the room. James nodded his head and smiled at the multiple camera angles as sweat began to assimilate at the crown of his head.

"No sweat," James whispered with a laugh and a sip of the ice cold water that sat in front of him.

There was a brief pause. Sasha motioned her hands towards someone backstage. Almost immediately, a small elderly woman came out and handed Sasha a blue envelope with bright red ink with the words "CONFIDENTIAL" printed largely on the front. Sasha then handed the envelope to Thomas.

"Your DNA results came in and we'd like to share them with

you, James," Thomas said.

"Alright. I'm ready," James said, trying to muster up some excitement for the cameras in a P.R. attempt to make Matador look favorable.

The four people looked into each other's eyes one by one as Thomas used a silver letter opener to guide through the seals.

"But first! James, I would like to know what it was like for you being adopted? Knowing that you were chosen by a loving family to give you a happy life. Did you ever suffer with any identity issues," Thomas asked, delaying the last bit of the envelope seal.

"Um. Uh... It never bothered me once I found out that I was adopted. My parents treated me like I was their own son. I think that's important with adoptions. A child can feel loved by anyone biological or not when they are in fact truly loved. Two of my children are fathered by someone else but I love them just as I do the one that came from my seed. I believe parenting is about being present, being kind, and being a leader," James said, staring into the camera.

"That's wonderful, James. Thank you for sharing. Are these principals those that you have shared with your own children," Thomas asked.

James paused for a moment, aware that his children's show WSS might be under scrutiny due to its popularity.

"Yes. I have. We all have choices at the end of the day. People choose what they want to be entertained by. People choose where to place their focus. There is revenue in having someone's attention," James finished, carefully eyeing each of the panel members.

"Therefore what you pay attention to could cost you. Is that right," Sasha added.

"Yes, you're right. WSS is like so many other shows. It's just entertainment. A few kids having some fun," James replied.

"Often at the expense of others, no? Would you say that more harm is done than fun," Sasha asked.

"I wouldn't say that. People nowadays are too soft. Too sensitive. They get bullied online and go crying on television shows about how they've been treated. Then someone donates a million dollars because their feelings got hurt. Someone gets fired for using a word. Another gets fired for a private conversation being taped and going viral on the internet. Just unplug the goddamn computer. Turn it off if there's someone inside of it that bothers you. We make things way too complicated due to the advances in technology. Matador for instance was created to make things EASIER," James concluded, using his hands the way an educator does to teach a class.

Pause. The room went silent for a moment as everyone eyed one another.

"I respect your point of view," Thomas began with a nod. "Now, when you were here a few weeks ago, we discussed nationality, DNA, epigenetics, racism, and how those factors influence our human experience," Thomas continued.

Leila interjected, "for instance, I am a Black American Woman. And some would say the African-American (Black People of the United States have no agency, no true home. We are born and raised in America, a country that does not treat us as equals. A country that consistently tells us to go back to Africa when we are tired of how we are treated here. But we are not African. Legally, Africa has no agency over what happens to us. They don't care. America doesn't care. We are treated as discarded people. The Filipino people who come here from their country have a country to go back to should they choose to. How can so many white Americans whose ancestors also come from across the seas, tell the Black people of African descent to go back to a country they've never set foot on?"

"Are you not African? Black, African, whatever. That's your country," James began.

"No. America is my country. I was born here. My father, my mother, their grandparents were born here. The slave owners who raped my ancestors and thus also became my ancestors were born here too. I am no less American than the person telling me to go somewhere I've never been," Leila continued.

The stage lighting appeared to get brighter, and hotter, as James West sat preparing to respond.

"I think what Leila is trying to say is that we are all American here, regardless of where our ancestors are from. And as a country we need more unity, peace, and equality. That's what we are doing here at Spread Love. We're excited that you're here with us to merge Matador as a means to broadcast this message to more viewers. Thank you again, Mr. West. Thank you so much," Sasha said, each word getting louder and happier than the last.

Enthusiastic applause erupted in the warm room breaking the necessary tension surrounding the panel speakers as well as the small audience.

"We all feel it's important to know where we have been in order to guide our steps to where we are going for a better future. Without further adieu, we have your DNA records from the labs," Thomas happily interjected. The blue envelope with bright red letters emerged again.

"Exciting," James responded, shaking his broad shoulders in an almost condescending tone.

Thomas slowly opened the seal, scanned his eyes over the documents, and handed the contents to James.

"What is this," James asked, with a bewildered look on his face.

"They're your results taken from your blood, saliva, and hair sample," Thomas responded.

"No. These can't be MY results. I'm not from any of these countries," James said.

"But these countries were found in your blood," Thomas continued.

"Morocco, Liberia… these are countries in Africa. I can see the Italian blood… but I am not African. This is some type of prank. I see what you people are up to," James said calmly laughing and tossing the paper to the table ahead.

"Those are approximations. It says more than just Africa, Mister West. But it appears that at least 60 percent of you is in fact… BLACK. Your parents… your biological parents.. Perhaps one of them was Black and the other biracial," Thomas argued, leaning in towards James.

"I do not believe this. I will not believe this. My skin is too light to be African," James argued, getting louder as the security officers nearby prepared to come closer.

"Sir, with all due respect, we… Black and African people come in various different shades. You are… we are… one race. The human race. Black people can be pale as powder or as dark as an abandoned desert sky. Your labs were sent and tested. No one has tampered with these results," Leila said with a satisfied smile.

James sat in silence, absorbing everything that he once thought about his existence. The life he lived because he thought he was a wealthy, caucasian man, impervious to the threats that many Black and African-American men had to face in America. Now, in front of thousands of people, it was confirmed that he was in fact Black.

CHAPTER TEN: THE PERFECT GIFT

Madrid, Spain

7:11 a.m.
Friday, May 4th

The sun rays shined directly onto Broc through the wooden blinds. Momentarily startled by a nightmare of being back in the altered augmented reality bullring with Matador Sebastian Barrio, he awakened and saw that his skin was still brown. A sigh of relief escaped his lips as his bare chest glistened in the dim bedroom. Broc tip-toed out of bed as not to wake Valentina.

Broc carefully walking through the apartment, reached the bathroom and stood there for many moments, staring into his own eyes and sizing up his entire reflection.

Head to toe, he was in a body that he once saw as a threat. He was in a body that he witnessed be treated unjust as he stood and did nothing because "It isn't my problem." Disgust for his actions and admiration for the beautiful artwork of God he had become were a dichotomy of interchanging emotions. Broc touched his own hair gently as he would the mane of someone who he was attempting not to wake. Broc slid his hands across his arms, then leaned over the bathroom sink, still gazing into his own eyes.

Broc turned on the cold water and splashed it upon his chiseled face. A smile washed over him as he met his eyes again, happy with what he saw.

A distant voice said, "Broc… come here, baby." Valentina had awakened and called out for him. The haunting piano sounds of 'Ow' by Stephan Moccio played in the foreground and got louder with each step Broc took towards the voice. A goddess stood in a grey silk gown at the entrance of the bedroom. He placed his hand under her chin and kissed her until all four of her lips were swollen with the rush of blood that excitement brings. Pressing his body to hers, she felt the sword between his legs and landed on the bed. Valentina untied Broc's shorts and placed his penis between her lips, landing on the back of her tongue. Broc let out sighs of pleasure accompanied by Valentina's moans of passion. The smacking sounds of her saliva guiding it's path up and down his shaft turned Broc on in a way he had never been.

Valentina's slow kisses felt like a million mouths all over Broc's muscular brown body, satisfying every urge he didn't know he had. Valentina opened her legs to let Broc's hands slide into her warm fortress of magic. The sensations between them were in rhythmic sync. This was the type of passion that makes a drug addict out of anyone. Valentina backed onto the bed, simultaneously lifting her gown over her head and throwing it on the chaise lounge. Broc stripped down to nothing and stood before Valentina staring into her big brown eyes and big brown breasts. Valentina widened her legs and with her index finger, motioned for him to "come closer".

Broc did as he was instructed and placed himself atop of Valentina as they moaned & growled in unison. Sighs of pleasure echoed in the Spanish decorated room. The Earth moved once he slid his veiny, stiff muscle into her wet abyss of wonder and creation.

The electricity between them was intoxicating. It was a welcome suffering of suffocation that neither of them wanted to end... The climax was coming. They both were coming... an orgasm that would arrive at the same time. Her lips began to shiver and shake on his dick... and then... that's when Broc saw a flash …

FLASH. FLASH. FLASH.

A familiar figure emerged between blinks of passion. Broc thought he saw Zinga instead of Valentina. He immediately jumped up to his naked feet.

"What's wrong, baby," Valentina asked, looking puzzled. Broc looked down at his skin again to make sure he was still who he thought he was and that the spell had not expired yet.

"I. I... don't know. I thought I saw something," Broc mumbled.

"You thought you saw what? Are you okay? You look like you saw a ghost. Your eyes are lost," Valentina whispered, sitting up with her excited nipples like sharp arrows aimed directly at him.

"Naah. I'm good... I just.. need a minute. I'm good. Promise," Broc said, slowly out of breath.

"Come here... It's okay," Valentina said, as she used her hand to sensually rub the vertical smile between her legs.

Broc laughed slightly, shrugged, and went back in between the walls of his fleshy, warm new home. The piano continued playing whilst guiding each stroke of their bodies colliding.

Two two of them lay with their eyes closed, tongue kissing... then playfully teasing, flicking, and touching tongues. Eyes closed.

Broc decided to open his eyes. There lay toothless, smiling Zinga. His penis was now inside of Zinga. Broc's eyes widened in horror. Zinga opened her eyes slowly and Broc shot to his feet, falling onto the floor in fear....

"What... Whaaatttt..." Broc whispered.

"Surprise," Zinga said as if she was asking a question.

Zinga stood up with her old Asian body naked.. and her ratted, draped clothes suddenly appeared and began to cover her body like a choir robe. Her colorful headscarf flew through the room onto her head, changing colors, blue, orange, and purple lightning bolts.

Broc stood up facing Zinga... as her face slowly started to

change again. Several faces flashed through her face as Broc stood in silent disbelief. Faces of women. Faces of men. Old. Young. Black. White. Asian. Moor. Beautiful. Ugly. Dark. Light.

Finally, the face of a middle aged white man emerged, donning a brown suit jacket and clothing that appeared to be very aged, vintage. The man looked Broc directly into his eyes and said, "I am Robert Ruffin Barrow. I am no negro. I am no slave. I am no nigger."

END SCENE.

"The only real voyage of discovery consists not in seeking new landscapes, but having new eyes." - Marcel Proust

FIGHT THE BULL.

THIS CONCLUDES SEASON ONE.

THIS IS THE END.

FOR NOW.

About the Author

Khalilah Yasmin is an author and poet. She has her Bachelor of Science in Psychology. With a keen interest in human behavior, she enjoys the dichotomy between art and psychology as a medium to alter perceptions. From Bellevue, Nebraska, Yasmin currently resides in Las Vegas, Nevada.

Twitter: @KhalilahYasmin

KhalilahYasmin.com

If you enjoyed MATADOR, please take a moment to write a review on Amazon. Even a short review helps and would mean a lot to me.

My intention is to create MATADOR into a film.

If you spread the word, you'll be a part of making my dreams come true.

Thank you.

Sincerely, Khalilah Yasmin

For Alexandria,
It's a pleasure
meeting you!

♡ Khalila
xox.

Made in the USA
San Bernardino, CA
18 October 2018